DEEP RED

PAUL KANE

SHORT, SCARY TALES PUBLICATIONS

BIRMINGHAM, ENGLAND

Published by
Short, Scary Tales Publications
15 North Roundhay
Birmingham
B33 9PE
England

www.sstpublications.co.uk

Book design by Paul Fry

First Edition: November 2018

10 9 8 7 6 5 4 3 2 1

Praise for *RED* & *Blood RED*:

'*RED* not only tips its hat to "Little Red Riding Hood," but "Peter and the Wolf," and "Who's Afraid of the Big Bad Wolf?" and every werewolf type motif in between . . . This time around Kane puts a twisted horror spin to it, with even a fair amount of social criticism thrown in for good measure . . . Kane does an incredible job of combining horror and humour into one tasty morsel.'
(*Cemetery Dance* Magazine)

'Kane expands on the "Little Red Riding Hood" mythos with a sharply-written novella that pits a descendent of the classic fairy tale character against the "real" creature of the same story. But make *NO* mistake: this isn't for kids! You can tell Kane had a real ball-twisting time updating "Riding Hood", especially in how he has crafted this new, psycho-sexual "wolf." For the sake of not ruining anything else, let's just say *RED* is a real BLOODY good time!'
(*Horror Fiction Review*)

'*RED* is a gleefully gruesome tale that moves at an excellent pace. Its length is a joy, reminiscent of a line from another fairy tale: "Not too big, not too small, just right." Paul Kane does a rip-roaring rendition of the *Red Riding Hood* story . . . He has the gift of summing up a situation in a sentence. *RED* is wonderfully written; it is easy to sink one's teeth into it and devour it with relish.'
(*Hellnotes*)

'This is a good scary story for those stormy nights or bright days. It is strong enough to terrify either way and will stay in your mind for days afterwards. Stories like this don't come along very often, as all readers know.'

'*RED* is bloody brilliant—clever, classy and bound to chill you to the bone!'

'Paul Kane has enriched the werewolf mythos with a seamless re-imagining of a hypnotically suggestive fairy tale, embellishing it with the harsh, alluring scent of an ages-old psychosexual predator who easily rivals that other undead villain from Eastern European folklore, the vampire. A relentless and grisly fairy tale for dark times, *RED* is filled with the blackest blood from the deepest parts of our bodies, and is thoroughly recommended.'

'I adored fairy tales as a small child, and I enjoyed reading *Blood RED*. Whilst being modern, it keeps returning in new and apt ways to the early version we know from the nursery, paying its dues while reinterpreting the tale in ways that will give you the shivers. And Kane is adept at putting flesh on the bones: all the more horrifying, my dear, when he strips it off again.'

'Pleasingly accessible, fast-paced and gloriously gruesome, *Blood RED* gives a fresh lick of paint (red, obviously!) to an old tale and adds a distinctly adult tone. Good fun.'

(Mark Yon, *SFF World*)

'I loved the twisted take on *Little Red Riding Hood*. Who doesn't love dark and twisted tales inspired by disturbing and unsettling fairy-tales? I loved every page. I had a great time reading *RED* and *Blood RED!*'

(5 * Review, *Book Lover's Boudoir*)

'One taste is all it will take to get you hooked, and after that, your thirst for the sweet *Blood RED* stuff that Paul Kane has to offer will undoubtedly be as voracious as any beast's.'

(A Girl's Guide to Horror)

'You cheeky bastard! Not only have you revamped the Robin Hood legend, now you have taken *Little Red Riding Hood* and turned what was already a dark fable into a descent into pure, action-packed horror . . . Thanks Paul!'

(*Zero Signal* Magazine on *Blood RED*)

Other Books by Paul Kane:

Novels
Arrowhead
Broken Arrow
Arrowland
Hooded Man (Omnibus)
The Gemini Factor
Of Darkness and Light
Lunar
Sleeper(s)
The Rainbow Man (as P.B. Kane)
Blood RED
Sherlock Holmes and the Servants of Hell
Before
Forthcoming: Arcana

Novellas & Novelettes
Signs of Life
The Lazarus Condition
Dalton Quayle Rides Out
RED
Pain Cages
Creakers (chapbook)
Flaming Arrow
The Bric-a-Brac Man
The P.I.'s Tale
Snow
The Rot
Beneath the Surface (with Simon Clark)

Collections

Alone (In the Dark)

Touching the Flame

FunnyBones

Peripheral Visions

The Adventures of Dalton Quayle

Shadow Writer

The Butterfly Man and Other Stories

The Spaces Between

Ghosts

Monsters

The Dead Trilogy

The Spirits of Christmas

Shadow Casting

Nailbiters

Death

The Life Cycle

Disexistence

Kane's Scary Tales Vol. 1

More Monsters

Forthcoming: Lost Souls

Editor & Co-Editor

Shadow Writers Vol. 1 & 2

Terror Tales #1-4

Top International Horror

Albions Alptraume: Zombies

The British Fantasy Society: A Celebration

Hellbound Hearts

The Mammoth Book of Body Horror
A Carnivàle of Horror: Dark Tales from the Fairground
Beyond Rue Morgue
Forthcoming: Dark Mirages

Non-Fiction
Contemporary North American Film Directors: A Wallflower Critical
Guide (Major Contributor)
Cinema Macabre (Contributor)
The Hellraiser Films and Their Legacy
Voices in the Dark
Shadow Writer – The Non-Fiction. Vol. 1: Reviews
Shadow Writer – The Non-Fiction. Vol. 2: Articles & Essays
Leviathan – The Story of Hellraiser and Hellbound: Hellraiser II
(contributor)
Hellraisers

Dedication:

For Angela Slatter, who loves the
dark fairy tale stuff as much as I do.

Acknowledgments:

My thanks to Paul Fry at SST for taking a chance, not only on the sequel to the original *RED* but allowing me to polish off the entire trilogy. A huge thank you to Barbie Wilde for agreeing to do the introduction, and to Dave McKean for the brand new excellent cover; the *RED* books would simply not be the same without his art on the front! As usual, hugs and massive thank yous to all my friends in the writing and film/TV world, for their continual help and support in the past. A very special thank you, though, to people like Clive Barker, Neil Gaiman, Stephen Jones, Mandy Slater, Amanda Foubister, Christopher Fowler, Stephen Volk, Tim Lebbon, Jason Arnopp, Kelley Armstrong, AK Benedict, Peter James, Mike Carey, John Connolly, Pete & Nicky Crowther, Simon Clark and so many more. The best mates anyone could hope for. Lastly, but never, ever leastly, a big words-are-not-enough thank you to my incredible family—especially my brilliant and hugely talented wife Marie. Love you guys so much.

A recap for the previous two *RED* books (WARNING, contains spoilers! If you haven't read these, both are included in *Blood RED*, also from SST Publications).

RED

Rachael Daniels is a lowly care worker, spending her days helping elderly clients in their homes—including Tilly Brindle, who is almost like family. Depressed because she's split up with her boyfriend, Rachael's best friend Steph takes her out on the town. But she's forgotten to give Tilly her medication, so ends up doing a mercy dash through the city at night to get it to her. Unfortunately a wolf-creature called Finch—who can change his appearance, but can be also be seen in reflective surfaces—is hunting the young woman and gets to Tilly first, taking her place to fool Rachael. In the resultant fight, it appears as if Rachael has killed the beast in the local park. However at the end, as Steph visits Rachael to see how she is—and it's revealed Tilly survived the ordeal—she, and we, discover the wolf actually won and ate Rachael, taking her form. Now Steph looks set to be its next victim . . .

Blood RED

In the aftermath of the events in *RED*, a team of trackers has shown up to kill the wolf—led by (Tom) Hunter, who wields a silver axe. At the same time a confused Rachael is wandering the streets, then returns home to find her mother has shown up. The girl breaks down, telling her she's had a nightmare about being eaten. During the course of his investigations, Hunter meets Rachael and there's an immediate attraction. However, wolf attacks keep happening—which might be her losing control of this new body she seems to have taken control of. As his team gets picked off one by one and more blood is spilt, including Rachael's mother, Hunter goes on the run with Rachael to keep her safe—still unaware of the truth about what she is. At a motel out of town, they sleep together, but as the police show up—including a rookie cop, Peel—it becomes clear another, female, wolf has been committing the murders. Flashing back in her mind to when Finch became The First Wolf, thousands of years ago in a cave, Rachael defeats him and finally takes full control of his body. In the confusion, Peel kills the distracted female wolf, though not before Hunter also loses his life. The finale shows that Tilly and Steph both survived and are infected with the wolf 'virus'. Not only that, Rachael is giving birth to the child she and Hunter conceived at the motel.

And now, the epic story concludes in *Deep RED . . .*

INTRODUCTION
BARBIE WILDE

F AIRY TALES ARE CURIOUS THINGS. I VIVIDLY REMEMBER MY MOTHER reading me 'Hansel and Gretel,' 'The Three Little Pigs' and of course, the seminal 'Little Red Riding Hood' when I was young. How were tiny tots supposed to go to sleep after hearing about flame-roasted kiddies as a witch's snack, or houses being violently destroyed by the single puff of a wolf's breath, or even worse, yet another wolf slaughtering a granny then wearing her skin and clothes to fool a young girl so he can feast on her tender flesh? Such charming little stories to send children off to dreamland.

Violence flows like a scarlet, subterranean river through the heart of many iconic fairy tales, so perhaps these stories were meant to warn children that the world can be a terrifying and dangerous place. That mummy and daddy wouldn't always be around to protect you. That shaping-shifting wolves and sweet little old ladies with unfortunate warts on their chins might actually want to devour you. The unrelenting grimness of Grimm's fairy tales was cautionary at the very least, never mind the gruesomeness of the *Jack the Giant Killer* and *Shockheaded Peter* stories.

With bedtime fables like these, no wonder human beings are so fascinated by horror. Not only have we been indoctrinated from a very early age; thousands of years ago we were sitting around campfires, shivering in bearskins, scaring ourselves to smithereens by recounting fearsome fantasies and believing that a giant wolf consumed the moon every month. (There's that 'lupine' motif again.) Today we read blood-curdling novels and go to horror movies, but the effect on our nervous systems is the same. It seems that it's in our DNA to be thrilled and, at the same time, repelled by horror.

Throughout Paul Kane's *RED* trilogy, I've been enthralled by Rachael Daniels' story—our modern Red Riding Hood—as she flees not only from the real life horror of the average human lowlife lurking around council estates, but from something else that is shadowing her—a mysterious creature that is snuffling out the familiar scent of a nemesis from the distant past and who is eager to taste the blood that was denied to it all those centuries ago. And in *Deep RED*, it's not only Rachael in danger, but her child as well—one that by all rights shouldn't exist at all. And the human race isn't doing so hot either.

From *RED*'s shocking first chapter through wicked twists and turns to the post-apocalyptic denouement of *Deep RED*, the saga will surprise, tantalize and beguile you. Kane's tense, powerful and expressive prose conjures up unsettling images in your mind that you won't be able to shake off for months. *Deep RED* is a gore-drenched, graphic tale populated with characters that you care about and empathize with, who are fighting an implacable and vicious ancient enemy. And in this reader's humble opinion, *RED*, *Blood RED* and *Deep RED* are so imaginatively written that they would all make deliciously frightening horror movies.

—Barbie Wilde (actress: *Hellbound: Hellraiser II*, author: *The Venus Complex*, *Voices of the Damned*, and co-screenwriter & co-producer: *Blue Eyes*)

PROLOGUE

I T WASN'T WISE TO BE OUT HERE ON YOUR OWN.

Not in the daytime, let alone this close to nightfall. But the trip had taken longer than expected, in spite of the fact nobody knew this landscape better. This Godforsaken land, with its husks of buildings, craters in the roads and jagged bits of metal sticking up out of the ground like uneven teeth. Like *their* teeth.

This world had become a warped reflection of them, in fact—as monstrous as the things that had taken over. It was hard to remember what life was like before, to be honest; especially for someone like Pat. Vague recollections, images mostly—of playing with a puppy out in the garden as the sun shone down. Of being given a chain with a cross on it by Mum that was still worn today. Of being lifted by two strong hands, planted on Dad's knee as he read a story out loud; a favourite fairy tale, one that could never, ever be true.

Or could it?

In any event, Pat had felt safe while the story was being read—knowing it was *only* a fable. And anyway Dad was there, he would never let anything happen. He was the one who checked under the bed, in the closet for monsters. Except, when the real monsters came along, there was nobody who could save them—nowhere that was safe. Pat had been very little when they took control, multiplying like rabbits. The authorities had tried to combat them, but stood very little chance. The war that followed hadn't lasted long, but the aftermath certainly did. The human race had barely survived it—barely survived their own solution to the problem, either, which hadn't really proved a solution at all. Had killed as many of their own kind as it did the mutts.

The monsters had survived. The monsters had *thrived* . . . Leaving pockets of humanity, of resistance to fight back the best way they knew how. Most of them gravitating towards this region. It had been a long time since Pat had felt safe, a long time since Dad's knee, since the story. He was long gone, same as Mum and the rest of the family. This was the only world Pat had ever really known, this scene as familiar as it possibly could be. Scavenging out here had done that, before Pat had been found—been taken in. Been set to work, scouting, delivering messages . . . Pat could go unseen, pretty much—not draw attention like a squad of soldiers. Slip between buildings, journey through this wasteland like a duck sails through . . . *used to* sail through water.

No ducks now. Very little water.

That was the idea, anyway. That was how it usually worked. And at only seventeen, some might argue Pat was *still* too young to be out here—out here alone—but at least there was a purpose to it now. Not just looking for the next crust of edible bread, the next can of cold beans, but making a difference; keeping the hopes of their people alive, and doing as much damage to those bastard hounds as possible in the process. Pat was a vital part of the resistance's efforts, a cog in a larger machine—but a necessary one. Take this mission, for example: to deliver important intel about stuff like the enemy's movements, about co-ordinated attacks. Pat didn't know the ins and outs of what it said, nor what might be done with it—that was all on a need to know basis. On coded sheets of paper in the messenger bag, along with a few essential supplies: a bottle of whisky for Colonel Alkins of Outpost 7B for one, a token of gratitude for her help with that skirmish on the border a couple of weeks ago. Now, that woman was a force to be reckoned with and no mistake—a proper battleaxe. You couldn't let the fact that she was pushing sixty fool you; at the opposite end of the scale. Alkins had killed more monsters than Pat had had hot dinners . . . or cold ones, come to that. What she wanted with that foul liquid, though, was anyone's guess. Pat had tried it once in the barracks, been given a sip by a trooper called Willis: "Here lad, knock it back. That'll put hairs on your chest!" It had burned all the way down, making Pat's eyes water. Willis had laughed at the shiver as it did and the coughing afterwards, slapping Pat on the back (though whether that was out of affection or he was just trying to stop the choking, Pat still didn't know).

The information couldn't be broadcast over the airwaves, in case the monsters were listening in—oh, they were clever ones, these. Not your average braindead savages. If they *had* been, maybe people would have stood more of a chance? Wasn't to say they weren't savage; they were that all right. Pat had witnessed enough bloodletting by those things to fill a thousand nightmares . . . not that people slept much these days, and not for more than a few hours at a time, if they were lucky. Pat definitely wouldn't be sleeping tonight, not even in the relative shelter of 7B. Too wired, too hopped up on adrenalin.

The trip back would be simpler, hopefully. Only reason it had taken so long on the way here was that feeling . . . The feeling of being watched, being followed; you learnt to rely on those kinds of senses out here. Didn't matter how careful you were, though, how much you covered your tracks—and remember, those bloody things were the *ultimate* trackers!—you could still find yourself in trouble. Find yourself being stalked.

Find yourself dead.

Hadn't been that far into this city either, when Pat first started to notice it. Movement out of the corner of the eye, but then nothing there when you looked. The fingering of that chain around the neck, something Pat did unconsciously whenever the nerves kicked in; an overwhelming urge to run, regardless of the fact that would be the worst thing to do. You panicked, you made mistakes. Better to keep cool and just fade into the background if you could. Losing the shadows would be better, of course.

Which is what Pat had been trying to do, either throw off the tail or lead them a merry dance away from 7B. Away from anywhere. Until you knew you were on your own again . . . Not a good idea to be on your own, but an even worse one to have the wrong *sort* of company. Pat would rather spend a lifetime alone than face that.

The claws, the teeth, the blood . . . So much blood. So much . . . red.

More memories, flashes of things that had happened to Mum and Dad. Pat fought them down, needed to concentrate on shaking off whoever . . . whatever was following. In one building, through and out into the next. Turn once, twice, double back and go down a different alleyway.

It took a while, but finally Pat was satisfied the tail was gone. Then, and only then, was it okay to carry on with the mission. But, of course, by that time what there was left of the sun—watery and weak in a muddied sky—was low on the horizon. It would be night soon. Pat considered the options: hole up and wait until morning to continue;

or put on a spurt and get to 7B, spend the night there. The latter was clearly the most attractive choice by miles, but was it the most sensible?

Sensible or not, that's the one Pat plumped for: plotting the alternate route from there before following it; pulling the hood up over close-cropped, spiky hair, head down and onwards. Once or twice, there was that feeling again; not quite enough to double back or even *turn* back, abort the mission completely. More that it drove Pat on to reach 7B regardless, to reach sanctuary. At least there were people skilled in the art of warfare billeted in that place. Pat knew the basics, was okay in a scrap, but wasn't a natural born fighter. A handgun and a knife were the only weapons brought on these runs—anything else would simply slow things down. Rifles slung over the shoulder, rocket-launchers? They just got in the way . . . 'Course, whether Pat felt the same way when confronted by those mutts was another matter: a pistol and a knife wouldn't be much use in a stand up fight. That was one scenario where running might actually be better; when the fight or flight instinct told you that if you didn't make a break for it, you'd be killed on the spot.

Not today. It wouldn't come to that today.

The enemy had been avoided, fooled even, and Pat was almost at the target destination. Hidden in what had once been the foyer of a museum, which Pat couldn't help thinking now stood only as a testament to what had happened—exhibits destroyed, paintings blackened by fire—was the entranceway to the outpost: a set of wooden double-doors, also ravaged by flames, almost hanging off their hinges. Behind these, Pat found a second set of metal doors, the real doors, which would have taken quite a lot of explosives to force open. It was on this that Pat knocked—the staccato rap that was a secret entreaty to be let in. But that was still only the first of several steps which would gain a visitor entrance.

"Identify!" wafted a gruff voice through the door. The speaker sounded as if he was on a different planet, not a few feet away.

"P 15022012," came the reply. The code for Pat's name and a birth-date; a means of telling who the caller was. It was unique for every messenger, couldn't be copied. It was possible, of course, for that code to be tortured out of someone, but that was why there were yet more checks to undergo before Pat was allowed inside 7B proper.

There was the sound of locks being turned, of bolts being drawn back. Then suddenly one of the metal doors opened up. Pat could see a faint, flickering light in there, enough to illuminate the steps in front. Steps leading down to the checking in point, below ground; but not to the outpost itself, which was even deeper. That was where most of the human race lived these days, under the earth. The barrel of an auto-matic rifle was almost immediately jammed in Pat's face.

"Whoa, easy there!" Pat's hands were already raised, there was no need for that. Or maybe there was. It was this level of security that kept outposts like 7B free of any kind of infection. Free of infiltration.

"Move inside," the man with the gruff voice ordered—and now Pat could see he was a guy wearing a beanie and fatigues. His nose was bent, broken at some point in the past, and there were stitches over his left eye; thick and black, like laces in a boot. Pat had to wonder whether the wound had healed a while ago and the man simply liked the way this looked. It would certainly make any human think twice about tackling him . . . maybe even one of the beasts as well. "Slowly," warned the man.

"'Kay, just watch what you're doing with that cannon. We're all on the same side here," said Pat. Though, of course, that was yet to be proven. To this guard, Pat might be just another one of those things.

Inside the door was another guard—standard practice, in case the first one should fall. This guy was a little younger, but no less rough-looking: the stubbled chin only adding to this. Pat had seen them both around before, just not to talk to—unlike Alkins—and not on guard duty. This man said nothing, just closed the door again, and covered the first guard while he searched Pat, taking away the gun and knife. Wouldn't be needed here in 7B. Not when they were deeper in, anyway. He took the bag as well, then motioned for Pat to remove the hood.

"Down the steps," said the first guard, pointing the way with the gun, past the torches on the walls. They left the second man by the door, as Pat was escorted to the final checking area. The one with the mirrors.

It was still the most effective weapon they had, the most useful tool—and something that not even the dogs with all their wit had been able to overcome. As old-fashioned as it was, this method remained the only sure-fire way to wheedle them out. Pat was virtually shoved into the arena, lit by more torches on the walls, and ordered to face first the reflective surface on the right, then turn to the one on the left.

The guard behind nodded, as a newcomer entered. A familiar face, lined with wisdom and expression, framed with silver hair. She was accompanied by two more guards, one on either side who'd escorted her from below. "Now, now," the woman said, pointing to the gun the broken-nosed guard held raised. "There's no need for all that."

"Colonel Alkins," said Pat, saluting. The colonel threw one back at the messenger, taking the bag that was handed to her and rooting around inside.

"Any trouble?" asked the woman.

It was better to be honest, as the colonel was like a human lie-detector, and Pat *had* been late reaching the outpost. "I . . . er . . . I thought I was being followed at one point, but managed to shake them off."

The colonel paused, one eye narrowing, scrutinising Pat. "You're sure about that, are you? That you lost the tail?"

Pat thought again about the uneasy feeling, hand going to the chain. "Yes . . . yes, I'm sure."

Alkins nodded. "Good. Because we don't want any nasty surprises, do we?"

"No ma'am," answered Pat.

"All right then . . . ah!" At first Pat thought the colonel had come across the whisky; that always brought a smile to her face. Instead, it was the plastic folder she took out—dropping the bag down on the floor. Pat heard a smashing sound, the whisky bottle breaking inside the bag. Hadn't she seen it in there?

"Colonel, there was—" Pat began, but was cut off by the raising of a hand.

Alkins was frowning as she rifled through the papers. "The code to these," she said, then waited.

What? Pat didn't have it, that wasn't her mission. It would come via another messenger; the colonel knew that but—

Pat was beginning to get that same sinking feeling. Began fingering the chain more furiously. Everyone was staying well away from the mirrors, had done even when Pat was being checked over. But it would only take a step to the left or the right to get a side on view.

Yet to be proven we're on the same side. . . .

"Well?" There was something strange about the colonel's expression now, those eyes a little too wide. The mouth a little too big. Pat turned and looked at the scarred soldier barring the way, who glared back, unblinking.

How many?

No nasty surprises.

Pat shuffled to the side, trying to do so as subtly as possible. Not making a very good job of it. "I . . . I don't—"

"Oh come along!" snapped Alkins, "we haven't got all day, boy!"

That was when Pat knew for sure. Not when the image in the mirror showed something else looking back that wasn't the colonel—a warped reflection . . . same as the guards on either side of her—but then: when the woman spoke a final time.

And those words from the story, the fable Pat's dad used to read, came drifting back: *What big eyes, what big ears . . . What big teeth . . .*

All the better to eat you with!

Not today. Not today . . . Fight or flight? Pat had to decide.

Why not a little of both?

No weapons, they'd been taken from Pat, but there was still the chain. A chain being fingered, being undone. A chain with a sharpened cross; a silver chain that was being unfurled and whipped around in the direction of the three people in front of Pat.

It swiped across the first soldier's throat, opening that up; then the colonel's face, drawing a line across both cheeks and the nose; before blinding the third guard, streaking across both eyes. All of them reached up to claw at their respective wounds. Injuries they hadn't been expecting, let alone been quick enough to prevent.

Then there was the torch. Pat reached up and flicked the naked flame off the wall, in the direction of the bag, where it met the leaking whisky with a whoosh.

Pat turned. There hadn't been time to check whether the scarred man was one of their kind as well, but it was a fair assumption and Pat couldn't take the risk. Didn't think twice. The chain was up and out once more, catching the guard across the hands and forcing him to drop his rifle. Didn't mean anything—might just have been the sharp-ness of the cross. But when Pat lashed out again, and the man caught it—grabbing the chain with both hands—smoke started to rise from his palms. Pat had no choice but to let go, yet at the same time reached for the knife tucked into his belt: the one he'd taken from Pat, sticking out handle first. In seconds that was free and being plunged into the guard's chest. He fell, a look of surprise on a face that was in mid-transformation. With a satisfied grunt, Pat snatched the chain back—but there was no time to grab the pistol he'd also taken.

Because the figures at the back were rising, pushing through the flames, and they were being joined by more from below. Not just the colonel then, not just these men, but the entire outpost had been compromised—which was another assumption, but one Pat had wanted to deny until now. It meant one more base was gone, had fallen to them. It meant Colonel Alkins was dead, as well. No time for sadness, though, no time to mourn her . . .

Now was the time for the 'flight' part of the plan.

Pat began back up the stairs, had almost forgotten about the other guard there with the stubble until he was coming down the stairs the other way, snarling. Timing it just right, Pat crouched and the man tripped, going straight over and falling headlong down the rest of the steps. Not only did that leave the way clear for Pat to open the door, it would also hinder the enemy in hot pursuit; literally, as a glance back told Pat that a couple were on fire. Now Pat was extremely grateful for the alcohol, gave a silent thanks that it had been Alkins' favourite tipple.

Locks were undone, the door open again, and Pat virtually fell out into the museum. Legs working, time for flight. Don't look back, don't look back . . . But Pat couldn't help it; couldn't help casting a glance over the shoulder to see them emerging from the doorway. One, two, three—more. And Alkins changing as she did so, a streak of silver all that was left of her hair colour, marking her out as different from the rest of the pack.

Pat sprinted into the street, looking left and right, looking for a way out of this. Somewhere to hide maybe? Although now they had the scent, they'd simply track that—unless Pat could mask it somehow? But no, better to try and lose them in this maze, fool them into going one way when you were going another. Put enough distance between them that scent wasn't an issue. A long shot, sure, especially with their noses, but better than admitting defeat. Better than admitting . . .

That you were dead.

That you had been ever since you set foot in the outpost, as dead as everyone else inside that place. Pat was being watched, being stalked. Being hunted. Could sense it, could feel it. And that hunt could only ever end in death.

Left, right, up one alley, down another. Might be able to lose them, might be able to . . . Then Pat realised what had actually been happening; instead of leading them away and confusing them, *they'd* actually been the ones doing the leading. Doing the herding. Blocking off one route, forcing Pat into another until—

It opened out in front, a large space, much larger than the checking one. Like those gladiatorial arenas of old, illuminated by a full moon that had just poked its nose out from behind a cloud. Pat skidded into the middle, and immediately tried to backtrack—but it was already too late. They were everywhere, forming a circle around Pat; dozens of them now, probably all the ones that had been in 7B waiting. No hiding in closets or under beds; the monsters were out in the open here. All changed, no need for subterfuge. All fur and teeth and red eyes. As red as the blood they were eager to shed.

Not today. Not today . . . But *yes*, it would seem: today. The time had come. No more flight, but Pat wasn't going down without more fighting—no matter how hopeless the odds were.

Knife in one hand, chain in the other.

Then . . . something happened. A flash, moonlight glinting off something. And one of the mutt's heads rolled towards Pat's feet. There was growling, as the rest of the pack reacted to this. But there it was again, flashing metal. Flashing silver, catching the moon; a swish here, a swish there. Whatever . . . whoever this was, they were fast—maybe even faster than the beasts. *Definitely* faster than them, because they were falling, dropping like flies. Claws were flashing as well, but not nearly enough; legs and arms were flying all over the place.

Blood was spraying everywhere as well, the figure moving from one to another, ducking and rising, the blade a positive blur. Pat watched, open-mouthed, until there was only one monster left. The one with the silver streak in its fur, the one who had pretended to be Colonel Alkins. It was clutching the papers in its paw, scrunched up now but still readable. It looked for a second as if it would attack—take revenge on this person who'd killed all of its troops. But then it seemed to remember what it was holding, the possibility of decoding whatever was in them.

And it ran, bounding off into the distance. Into the blackness.

Leaving only Pat there. Pat and the man. His shoulders were rising and falling, just as he had been a moment before. He looked over to where 'Alkins' had vanished, perhaps thinking about going after her, but instead turned and faced the person he'd saved, a little out of breath. It was only now that Pat saw what the weapon had been: it was a perfectly polished silver axe (battleaxe vs battleaxe, if Alkins had stayed) which even now he was cleaning, wiping off the grue. It was as beautiful as it was deadly, that weapon, and for a moment it was all Pat could see. Then the rest of the man came into focus.

He was wearing dark cargo trousers and boots, his long coat coming down past his knees, over a jumper that had holes in it. He was bearded, and—like the Alkins creature—that was also shot through with silver-grey. There was a patch covering his right eye, long hair poking out from beneath a wide-brimmed hat. The figure took a step towards Pat, who involuntarily raised the chain and knife. Just because a person was human—and that was yet to be established here; Pat had been fooled once that day—didn't mean your intentions were good. Especially if you were out here alone, when you really shouldn't be.

"Relax," said the man, lifting the axe and resting it on his left shoulder, "I'm not going to hurt you."

Pat said nothing in reply.

"They got there way ahead of you. Saw 'em skirt round you, while you were trying to throw them off the first time."

Saw. . .? Then they hadn't been the only hunters out there observing Pat; this man had been responsible for at least some of those feelings. That sense of being followed.

"What's your name?"

Pat still said nothing.

The man laughed. "I'll tell you mine if you tell me yours."

"P-Pat . . . It's Pat."

"That short for Patricia, then?"

Pat frowned. How had he known that? Alkins had, she'd confided in her, but no-one else here. It had been the final reason Pat had suspected her doppelganger.

"*We haven't got all day, boy!*"

"Because it sure as hell ain't Patrick."

He drew closer, bending, holding out his free hand. Pat tucked the chain in her pocket, reluctantly accepting the shake. Then she looked around again at the devastation; at so many dead hounds. "How . . . how did you. . .?"

"Practice," replied the man. "Been doing this a long time. Probably even before you were born, girl. Getting a bit slow in my old age, actually."

Her face soured and she let go of his hand. "Don't call me that."

"What? Girl?" She nodded. "Okay, before you were born, *Pat*."

The mention of her own name reminded her that she still didn't have his. "I told you mine . . ." she prompted.

"Eh? Oh, right." He laughed again. "It's Peel," he told her. Then he turned his back on Pat, began to walk off. She watched him, gaping, and suddenly blurted out:

"Wait!"

He stopped, looked over his shoulder—and waited. Pat just stood there staring at him. The stranger sighed then, and said, "Yes?"

"Where . . . where are you going?"

He grinned at that and pointed in the direction the Alkins beast had fled. "Goin' hunting," was the answer, and he turned back around again and carried on.

"Wait!" Pat repeated and rushed to catch him up, to fall in step with him. He glanced across, but said nothing. "Who *are* you?" she asked again, not wanting his name this time; wanting the rest.

"It's a long story," he told her.

"Tell me," she said as she hurried to keep up with his strides.

As this man who'd saved her, who she'd only just met, led her away from the field of conflict. From the slaughter. From the pools of blood that looked almost black in the light from the moon.

But were in fact red. A deep, deep shade of red . . .

CHAPTER ONE

SHE WAS STILL RUNNING.

As fast as she could, arms out in front to bat away the foliage. Escaping through the woodland, through the dense green that surrounded her: the safe path nothing but a distant memory. Breath coming in short bursts, hardly daring to look at what was behind her. Hardly daring to remember what had happened in case she might break down and cry. End up standing stock still when she should be running through—

The estate at night, through streets that were barely lit. Away from what had occurred back there in the small flat . . . No, that wasn't how she'd escaped. She'd . . . There'd been a vehicle, a van of some kind. A young lad called Peter and she'd been—

Running, back to the motel room. Not away from the chaos this time but towards it, back to try and save the one man she'd loved more than anything in this world. Tom. Hunter. The man she'd just spent the most magical night of her life with except he was—

Back at the cabin, where her Gramma had met her end. Blood everywhere; red everywhere. He'd bought her the time to escape, to flee. Used that axe of his to distract the creature who'd been pretending to be her kin. Sacrificed himself so that she could get away, only the thing had chased her anyway once it was done with him. Chased her through the woods, through the generations, until it found her again. Until she'd come back full circle to the cabin, the flat, the motel room. So long ago, and yet no time at all. Different lives, different times.

It was almost time . . .

All so confusing, so *confused*. A jumble in her mind. The only thing she was certain of was that she had to run, to get away before—

No, wait, she'd won! She'd defeated the creature . . . hadn't she? That's what she thought. Yes, she'd defeated him—taken the monster on and beaten the thing. Only for the whole world to go to Hell after that, their progeny taking over.

She hadn't stopped anything, hadn't really won at all. The only good thing to come out of all this was—

Run! Run Little Red, as fast as you can!

And she was, again, through the green with something chasing her. How could it be chasing her when it was dead? When she'd killed it?

Already dead, just too stubborn to admit it. Too afraid.

Should she risk a glance, just a peek? She shook her head, she didn't want to see because then she'd know for sure. Then she'd have to admit it to herself. That she was losing control, losing her grip. Losing her . . . mind? It was a wonder that hadn't gone a long time ago. Sometimes, moving from place to place—running again—she had to wonder whether she'd already gone stark, staring mad. Wonder whether this wasn't all some dream, some nightmare she was unable to wake up from. On the run from the authorities, from people she owed money to, from . . . everyone.

Running, always running. Perhaps that was it, she'd been doing that for so long she didn't know how to stop.

You have to make sure, she said to herself. *Take a look and make sure there's nothing behind you, nothing following. Make sure you're safe.*

So she did. She turned, then let out a breath this time—not because she was exhausted, but through sheer relief. There was nothing out in the darkness, in that dark green through the branches. Nothing following, nothing hunting her.

Then she saw it: Red.

A red spot, a crimson circle. Only small, but it was there. A single red . . . No, not single. There were two of them now, quite close together. A *pair* of eyes; glowing red eyes. She almost screamed. It was still behind her, was still following after all these years. Wasn't possible, it couldn't be possible! She'd—

Two more of them appeared, not far away from the first set. As if they'd only just sensed her, only just spotted that she was ahead of them. Moments later another pair of eyes opened, then another, and another.

She wanted to scream now, long and loud. Wanted to scream at them to stay away, but no matter how hard she tried she couldn't find her voice. Ten, twenty, thirty . . . she was losing count now. So many eyes out there in the woods, just staring at her. There were more eyes than trees now, surely? Just watching her intently, waiting for . . . for what? For her to make some kind of move; to even twitch. And then they'd be on her.

They'd strike.

Was she going to give them that satisfaction? Let them just have her? Shouldn't have stopped running, should just have kept going.

But it wasn't too late, was it? She could turn and start again, try and escape. And that's just what she did, whirling around as fast as she could, facing front again . . .

Except the eyes were there as well. Ahead of her as well as behind. The future and the past. There was no escaping them, there never had been. That had been the real dream, thinking she ever could.

Quickly she looked left and right. Of course they were there as well, the red orbs securitising her, boring into her.

She had seconds, if that. Had to think of a way out of this. Not just stand there trying to cry out, letting them devour her. Like the last time. Like one of their kind had, although that bastard had regretted it in the end. Okay, let them come—she'd fight them. As weak as she was, she'd—

That was when they struck. All of them, all at once. Descending on her, tearing into her with claws and teeth. Ripping her limb from limb, the pain incredible.

She screamed then. The longest and loudest scream she'd ever managed in her life.

Screamed until . . .

. . . suddenly she opened her own eyes, right here, in the real world. If you could call it that. Screaming at the faces that surrounded her, that always did, day after day after day.

Faces that, more often that not, also had glowing eyes. Glowing eyes that were a deep shade of red.

&

He was surrounded, those red eyes out there in the darkness.

Not just him, but the others who had managed to escape as well. Trooper Andrew 'Angel' Southland (named by his mother, who always called him her little Angel) looked about him at what actually remained of those survivors. He could count them on the fingers of two hands . . . barely. All that was left of an outpost which had boasted more than fifty people, most of them fighters like himself; thank Christ there hadn't been any children at that station! Nobody had been expecting the sneak attack, there had been no warning—their lookouts killed before anything could be done to raise an alarm.

They'd come through the back way, through an underground system they shouldn't even know about. Clawing left and right, biting and ripping apart anyone who stood in their way until the walls were painted with blood. Forcing the humans there to the surface, into the twilight, where more of their kind were waiting. Angel had been proud of the way his men had fought, in those close quarters beneath the ground, then on the surface; facing an overwhelming number of mutts.

A massacre, that's what this was. An attempt—a successful one—to totally obliterate 5C. To wipe it off the face of the Earth. He and those who'd crawled away from there, others giving them covering fire— sacrificing themselves so that they could escape—had run. Though he wasn't leader material or anything, Angel had taken charge of the rag-tag team that was in total disarray; no sergeants, captains or majors left to dish out orders. And they'd tried to get away, only to be chased down the war-torn streets. Their enemy had finally cornered them near a park, where there was really only one place to attempt a last stand: a burnt-out bus. With a nearby bit of metal, Angel had levered open the emergency door at the back (if ever anything counted as an emergency, it was this) and ushered the others inside, waving his arm furiously until there was only him left. Then he'd joined them as they'd taken up positions at the windows—or what had once been windows at any rate. Relieved of their glass, they at least made decent gun placements.

It was from one of those that Angel now witnessed the approach of the dogs. He rushed to the other side of the bus, saw they were there too. A quick glance through the back and front 'windows' also confirmed that they were circling the old vehicle. There was no way out, he and the survivors were surrounded—just like in those old westerns he used to watch with his brother. An older brother who'd been killed in one of the first waves of attacks when those freaks rose up. The passing thought made him mad, chased away the fear momentarily.

"Pick your targets," he called to the other troopers in the bus, knowing they only had a limited amount of ammo left. "Make every shot count. And let's make these sons of bitches—"

That was where the speech ended, cut off when the wolves—as one—made their move. When they sprang towards the bus and his people began shooting. Some of the silver bullets hit their marks, Angel's included as he hunkered down and joined them in firing at the sea of fur. But it hardly dented their numbers, more hounds taking the place of their fallen comrades pretty much immediately.

There was a scream, and Angel looked across in time to see one of the troopers get dragged through a window. The top half of his body vanished, leaving khaki legs kicking out, so hard one of the man's boots came off and was flung back into the bus to bounce off a seat. Then the legs just stopped moving, collapsing against the window as a jet of redness sprayed inside.

Angel put up a hand, stepping back to avoid the blast of warm liquid—only to nearly slip on the floor which was already slick with it.

More screams, as troopers at other windows were killed one by one. Angel couldn't tear his eyes away as a clawed fist punched its way through one soldier's head, deflating it like a balloon; the meat and bone hardly slowing it down.

One trooper had his rifle wrenched from him and broken in two, such was the strength of these creatures. Then the muzzle end was rammed into its owner's chest, like he was a vampire being staked.

Bit by bit, the anger had drained from Angel to be replaced by fear again. The self-preservation thing that had urged these people to follow him, away from the main battle. But there was no way out, not now. Maybe not ever. There were just three of them left now, the others—only one of which he recognised, as a trooper called Harrison— had joined him, were even looking to him to get them out of this. Impossible! They were doomed . . . Not just the trio of survivors, but the human race. How could they ever have hoped to succeed against those things to begin with, when not even the governments, the *real* armies hadn't stood a chance? The most they'd been able to do was survive . . . for a little while anyway. Hope to see another dawn once night fell.

Now Angel knew that he definitely wouldn't—that he'd be joining the other angels very soon—a kind of peace washed over him. He wouldn't have to struggle anymore, rail against all this. Wouldn't have to live in fear, waiting for the other foot to fall every day. For him, it would be over. No more fighting, no more battles . . .

As the wolves flooded into the bus, he abandoned all hope and just waited for the inevitable.

But he was wrong to do so.

At the very last minute, perhaps even the last second, he heard it. The sound of engines. All the mutts that were inside the bus, that had been approaching Angel and his colleagues, eying them up as their next meal, paused, sniffed the air, then turned at the same time.

The wolves that had been climbing all over the outside of the bus were suddenly being scraped off, like he'd seen his dad scrape ice from the car during those harsh winters back in the day. No, not scraped so much as *blown* off—or more accurately torn into by a gun more powerful than anything they possessed to combat the enemy. The noise was incredible!

The ones inside exited, in support of, or in solidarity with, their kind; Angel didn't quite know, didn't care. But they ended up suffering the same fate. He rushed to a window and saw one of them get ripped to pieces by bullets that looked like miniature flaming arrows. Then Angel traced the fire back to a vehicle that had pulled up just off to the right of the bus, an open-backed pickup with a mounted machine gun at the rear that had ceased pumping out its deadly load for a moment.

"Deepak!" he heard someone shout, then traced that back to a man wearing a cap, riding a motorcycle which pulled up alongside the truck. "Concentrate your fire over there, into that clump of them! Ridgeway, go and check the bus for any survivors."

Angel saw one of the men from the pickup, keeping his head low all the time and clutching his helmet, rush across to the bus, forcing his way inside through the front doors this time. He clocked the three of them left, nodded, then said: "I think this might be your stop, fellas. Everybody out!"

Angel let the others go first, then followed the man called Ridgeway himself as they half-crouched, half-shuffled towards the truck. There were still plenty of the mutts around, enough to over-power them all—enough to overrun Deepak and his gun. They weren't out of the woods yet, by any stretch of the imagination. But Angel had started to hope again.

"Get in, get in," Ridgeway told them, doing the same thing Angel had done when they'd found the bus—waving the survivors into the back of the pickup this time. He stopped for a second, raised his rifle and let off several bursts, felling a number of the creatures that had gotten too close for comfort.

The cap-guy on the bike was shouting orders at his team, telling them to get moving—that he would hold the enemy off, lead them away. Angel's first thought was: *Is he crazy?* Then he took in the man, properly took him in now he was closer. There was a calmness about him that had nothing whatsoever to do with letting go of life, of giving up. Quite the opposite in fact: it came from embracing it, and all the confidence that went with that.

Here was a bloke who hadn't just had the mantle of leadership thrust on him; he looked like he was born to it. And he was about to pull all of their arses out of the fire, as young as he appeared to be . . . Twenty? Twenty-one, if he were a day.

"*Go!*" he shouted to Ridgeway, to his driver, and even slapped the side of the truck to emphasise they should get motoring. As they pulled away, Angel watched—the hounds now massing behind the biker. Watched as the man dragged the front of his bike up into the air, spinning on the back and taking out the nearest couple of wolves with his front wheel.

When it hit the floor again, he set off, trailed by a horde of the beasts. Not one of them came after their vehicle. The guy was leading them away like the Pied Piper of Hamelin, off into that park.

Angel realised his mouth was hanging open and he closed it again. He wasn't quite sure what had just happened; how he was still alive. "He . . ." All he could do was point back towards the biker. Finally, he found the words, staring at Ridgeway. "It's suicide. They'll slaughter him!"

The soldier shook his head. "I seen him get out of tighter spots than that, man. He'll be okay." Then Ridgeway smiled. "It's down to him we came looking for you in the first place. We should have been scouting out a route for a supply run . . . But he had a feeling something was wrong at 5C."

Angel was gaping again, blinked once, twice. "How did. . .?"

"Look, don't ask me. But I've been around long enough to know you trust that guy's instincts, right?" There was a look in Ridgeway's eye that told him this man had been saved by those instincts, probably more than once. Angel was still new to the experience though.

"But who. . .?" asked one of the other soldiers this time, for variety; Harrison he noted.

Ridgeway beamed once more, as the truck hit a bump in the road and jolted them all; as they passed what was left of a street sign that read 'nham Estate'. He adjusted his helmet and regarded them all in turn, though Angel knew who that had to be back there. Even at 5C they'd heard the rumours, the stories. He hesitated to use the word legend, but if the cap fitted . . . It could only be one person at the end of the day. But Jesus, he was so, *so* young.

"That folks . . . that was—"

"Daniels," Angel finished for him. "It was Tommy Daniels, wasn't it."

Ridgeway nodded, grinning again and clapping Angel's shoulder. "The one and only, my friend. The one and only."

CHAPTER TWO

"**H**OW'S THE GRUB?"

Peel looked up to see the young girl called Pat standing in front of him. No, not girl—he wasn't allowed to call her that. Young *person*, then. Much better. She was holding a tray with a bowl and cup on it, hovering around the seat opposite him. Peel held his hand out for her to sit, then spooned more of whatever it was he was eating into his mouth. Could well have been mashed up grubs for all he knew; looked like it; smelled like it too. But it actually tasted okay, and he wasn't complaining.

"S'good," he said to her, and she smiled as proudly as if she'd made it herself.

"Told you." Pat began to shovel her own mixture into her mouth, inhaling it practically, pausing only to take swigs of an equally unidentifiable liquid from her cup. It was something he'd seen before, though not for a long time. Grabbing food and drink when you could. Eating quickly, because you never knew when you might get another meal—or even if you'd be able to finish the one you had.

Looking around him, though, Peel reckoned she'd be okay in here. The amount of soldiers present; how far they all were underground. But then she'd grown up out there, where he'd existed for so long. He'd at least had experience by the time everything hit the fan, couldn't even imagine what she'd gone through as a kid out in the wilds, surviving until she was picked up by these people. She'd told him about some of it, broad strokes, but he could imagine the rest. Pat had been more interested in his story, really.

It was an unusual one, had to be said. So as they'd gone off tracking the wolf that got away a couple of nights ago, and after much pestering, he'd filled her in on the background. Didn't seem any reason not to, wasn't like it was some big secret or anything. In a way, it had been nice to tell someone about it. Nice to have the company as well. It had been a while since Peel had talked to *anyone*.

As he'd spoken, memories had come flooding back. Of leaving school, training to be a policeman just like his cousin had been; the one who'd died in mysterious circumstances during that business up in Norchester, which he always suspected had been covered up. Making constable then and waiting to be in the right place at the right time to investigate something big. And boy, had that come along—couldn't have been any bigger, in fact.

First, those murders on the Greenham Estate. It had been put down to gangs initially because of the location; that place was always blowing up. But then more incidents had occurred, like the massacre in that nightclub (and he'd had to explain here to Pat what those were, because she'd never seen—let alone been in—one; "It's the kind of place you'd be hanging around in on a Friday and Saturday night at your age," he'd said, "if things hadn't gone to Hell in a handbasket."). He'd never seen anything like that crime scene, and neither had his superior, Moss. Body parts everywhere, blood everywhere. Commonplace now, sadly, but back then it had been pretty shocking. And eyewitnesses mentioning some kind of large dog, which chimed with a few of the statements from Greenham.

It had been a dog, all right, as he'd discovered himself later on.

He'd been there when the case started to come together, when they'd discovered the couple who seemed to be at the centre of it all— the attacks, the murders—and who they traced to a motel outside town. Peel had gone along with the big boys, with the armed response units, with his colleagues, in the middle of all the action. A takedown, an honest to God takedown, and he was going to be involved in it all—on the front ranks! Right place at the right time. Looking back, he couldn't believe that he'd actually been excited about it. Thought it would be fun! Operation 'Dogcatcher' they'd called it, because they were entertaining some bizarre notion that the bloke was training ferocious animals to do his bidding. Christ . . .

The slaughter which followed, when they'd surrounded the chalet that couple were in, had been the worst thing he'd ever seen in his life. And the most surreal. He'd watched as Moss had turned into . . . something. Knew now it was one of those bloody mutts he'd devoted his entire life to tracking, to killing—but at the time he hadn't had a clue what was going on. Didn't know that it had killed his governor and taken his form, to infiltrate the group of police officers and cause maximum carnage. That the couple weren't actually running this freakshow at all, they were running *away* from it, like he should have been doing if he'd had any sense.

It had taken them all by surprise, the bloodshed that ensued. Officers cleaved in half, heads flying in the air. Flying . . . just like he'd done when that explosion happened, rolling the car he was in. Waking up, he'd surveyed the devastation and heard the cries coming from that motel room. Scrambling out of his upturned vehicle, he'd made it back there, grabbed a discarded rifle, and filled that hairy fuck full of lead . . . At least he'd assumed it was lead. Turned out the gun had been filled with silver bullets, or he might not have made it out of that situation alive either.

There had been only two survivors of that night, him and the girl—her boyfriend having taken the thing on and paid the price. Problem was, the beast had reverted back to its human form by the time the authorities made it to the scene. Peel had done quite a bit of damage to it, made sure it was dead in fact by emptying the entire magazine into the body even after it had been felled, but in that state even he could tell it was female. Not a dog, not a wolf, but a woman *he'd* shot and killed.

There had been questions, of course, but the girlfriend had been practically useless. Refused to back up his side of what—admittedly—had sounded like a crazy story. How could one woman have torn through all those coppers, let alone the armed ones? She was a what? A wolf? Pull the other one! Then the girl had vanished, left him holding the can, and he'd been drummed out of the force. He always suspected there were those who believed him, however. The same folk who'd hushed up what happened to his cousin, who couldn't let shit like that get out because it would cause a mass panic. Maybe it should have done, because when what happened happened, none of the public had been prepared for it at all. When those things rose up and started to take over, nobody had any hope of defeating them. Not even the muppets who *thought* they had a handle on it.

In the meantime, as he had done that night when he'd saved Pat, Peel had gone hunting. His little contribution to the cause, in an effort to thin the herd. But he'd been one man, alone, trying to stem the tide of something that would, in the end, wash over them all. He'd had his successes, saved a number of other lives in his time—lives that had probably been lost again once the chaos reigned—but in the end he was only ever going to win the battles, not the war. Afterwards, he'd simply carried on doing what he knew best, what he'd trained *himself* to do best. Hunt those furry arseholes, then take them out. One by one if he had to. Peel hadn't been able to stop the world from becoming theirs, but he could avenge it. And maybe one day . . .

He'd shaken his head at that, sighed. Had been surprised when he looked down and saw Pat's hand in his as they walked.

"It's what we've been fighting for as well," she'd told him then with a smile. This kid who'd grown up in fear of her life every single day; who'd almost been savaged by wolves that had killed her friends back at the outpost; who still hadn't given up hope, who still had faith every-thing would work out. "*All* of us. Let me show you."

She'd persuaded him to return home with her—the only one she'd known for some time. To give up on the hunt . . . for now. Pat still had to report back about what had gone down, and he looked like he could use a kip and some decent food.

"Come on. It's safe there, honest."

So, reluctantly, he'd agreed. Checking to make sure *they* were not being followed—that they weren't being hunted themselves—she'd taken him back with her. To the base she had set out from to deliver her message. A base that made 7B look like a hovel, apparently. It was a bit of a trek, to the outskirts of the city through territory that had once been parks and woodland—an attempt to bring some colour and nature to an urban environment—but was now all scorched earth and stumps. Along the way they passed burnt out houses, one which would probably have been quite a nice cottage back in the day. Peel glanced in through the shattered windows and saw only the remains of furniture now, bookcases on their sides and a few scattered photographs. All that was left of the owners.

Eventually, however, Pat stopped and pointed. "That," she'd said, "that is 1A."

"What? *That*? A lump of rocks?" What his old mum might have called crags on a bank holiday day out, it looked just as out of place here as the grass and trees must have done. Just as battered as well, blackened and cracked in places; the edges worn not by time but by a relentless hail of missiles. Pat shook her head, and approached the structure with her hands in the air.

Almost immediately, several red dots appeared on her person. "Hold your fire. P 15022012 reporting," she called out.

"You're late returning," came an electronic voice from somewhere, echoing as it spoke. "And who's that with you?"

"Ran into some trouble," Pat replied, thumbing back. "He helped me out of it." She motioned for Peel to come forwards now and he did so, but kept his hands where they were, holding his axe, in spite of the fact those laser dots had found his body. "I can vouch for him."

There was a long pause, during which Peel almost bolted. Then the voice came again: "Proceed!"

Pat began to walk forwards, toward that solid wall of rock in front of her, still beckoning him to follow. Frowning, he did so, wondering what they were going to do when they eventually reached it. Then he took another step and suddenly it all vanished, replaced by a black hole in the surface. The entranceway to a cave.

"Wha. . .?" He looked over at Pat, who couldn't help smirking. Peel stepped back again, and all he could see was the rockface. Forwards another step and the opening returned. "A projection," he stated, and she nodded, pointing up ahead.

They entered the cave, which seemed to go back much further than the rocks would allow, dipping slightly Peel thought. Until they came upon an archway and a set of metal doors.

"This is all a bit James Bond, isn't it?" he said to nobody in particular.

"Who?"

"Never mind." The doors opened then and he started.

"Come on," Pat told him, taking his hand again and leading him inside. But not far, as another set of closed doors were blocking their progress this time. Then the ones behind them suddenly closed again. A bright white light illuminated the space, a room of about twenty foot square, polished surfaces surrounding them, throwing back their reflections whichever way they turned. If the dots and the voice outside, the projection, had been the first line of defence, this was surely the next: a way of wheedling out anyone pretending to be something they weren't. Peel looked up and spotted a camera in the corner, observing it all.

There was a jolt, and he felt his stomach lurching. Though he had no other way of proving it, Peel knew they were descending; realised this was some kind of lift they were in rather than a porch or a room.

Down they went, and down. Deeper and deeper until he thought they were never going to stop. When they eventually did, the doors in front still didn't open. Instead, a blue light replaced the white one, which scanned them both from top to bottom.

When it was done, a more normal light returned and a different voice—a woman's voice—said: "Please place all weaponry in the opening provided."

Peel looked about him, but couldn't see anything. Then a flap dropped to his right, which looked like it should lead to a laundry chute. Pat placed her knife in there, the only weapon she was carrying, then waited for Peel to put his axe inside. Sighing, he did so reluctantly, and folded his arms—waiting with her.

"*All* weaponry!" the voice clarified, and it was then he knew the scan had been some kind of X-ray. Peel fished about under his coat, taking out a couple of pistols, then produced a series of his own knives from about his person—including one strapped to his calf. He put each one in turn into the hole.

"Cleared," said the voice.

It was only now that the other set of doors in front of them opened up into a sealed off corridor. At the far end Peel saw what looked like two cannons mounted on the wall, which followed their progress as they walked down towards yet another set of doors: one in front and one off to the side.

"Don't take any chances, do they?" said Peel.

"I'm sorry," replied his companion in an apologetic tone.

"No need. I like that. You let your guard down, take your eye off things for even a moment . . . And, well, you're inclined to lose it." He reached up to tap his eye-patch and the cannon on his side shifted position, locking on with a cocking sound.

"No sudden movements please," the female voice warned.

"You could have told me that before," Peel shouted up to her.

When they reached the end of the corridor, the door slid open on Peel's side. "You need to go through there now," she told him. "I'll see you in a little while."

"Why, what's going to happen to me?" asked Peel, but already she'd stepped through the door which had opened in front and closed almost immediately behind her. He shrugged. "In for a penny . . ."

After he stepped through his own doorway Peel was greeted by yet more guns, this time wielded by two burly men in uniform. "Howdy," he said, nodding to each in turn, but they said nothing back. With his rifle, one of the soldiers motioned for Peel to start walking and he was taken to a small room then told to strip. "Hey now, come on. Leave a guy with some dignity, yeah?"

The soldier's answer to that was to raise his rifle slightly and repeat the 'request'. Sighing, Peel began to undress, starting with his hat. "Aren't you two even going to turn your backs for Heaven's sake?" They didn't, but one held out a clear plastic bag for him to put his clothes into.

When he was completely naked—they insisted he had to take everything off, including his boxers and even his eye-patch—he stood there covering his modesty with his hands, shivering, and both of them left, the door closing behind them. Seconds later he felt a drop of water from above. Peel looked up, saw another. Then another. A shower cranked up then, the water it sprayed him with freezing cold. He shuddered, but once he'd gotten over the initial shock actually started to enjoy the sensation; the liquid running down him, dripping off him. Peel couldn't remember the last time he'd actually *had* a shower. Probably in some flea-bitten hotel somewhere while he'd been chasing down yet another flea-bitten hound.

Nowadays, if you even had water you preserved it. You lived off it. Although perhaps it was recycled here? It was quite a set-up after all.

The water stopped abruptly then, interrupting his thoughts, and in its place air was now blowing into the room. It was like a giant hand-drier they used to have in public toilets, and in seconds he was no longer wet at all.

More doors opened up, on a larger room in front of him. A woman was standing in the middle. She was quite striking, her auburn hair tied back in a ponytail, and she was wearing a white coat. On the table next to her were various medical instruments, some of which looked more like torture devices. Peel's hands instinctively covered himself up again.

She gave a small laugh. "I assure you, there's nothing down there I haven't seen before, Mr . . ."

He could feel his cheeks burning red. "P-Peel," he told her. "Just Peel."

"I'm Dr Kingsley. Now, it probably doesn't need saying, but there are guards just outside who'd be in here like a shot if you caused me any trouble. But you don't look the type to me." She grinned, then said: "So, come along now, Mr . . . Come along, Peel, don't be shy. Let's have a good look at you, shall we?" And that's exactly what she did. During the course of the next hour or more, there wasn't an inch of him she hadn't had a 'good look at' by the time she was finished. He hadn't been poked and prodded like that since his medical to get into the police force.

"How did this happen?" Dr Kingsley asked at last, pointing to the empty socket where his right eye had once been.

"How do you think? Fighting one of those fu . . . those mutts out there."

"It took the eye out?"

Peel shook his head; he knew what she was driving at. If the wolf had clawed out his eye, it could well have infected him with the virus that had turned all the others. "Evasive manoeuvres," was all he'd say.

She nodded. "Well, I'm pleased to inform you you're in pretty good nick, Peel, all things considered. Almost finished now—we just need to get your bloods done. Make doubly sure there isn't anything nasty lurking." Dr Kingsley took out a needle.

"There isn't," he assured her. "And I gave at the office."

She chuckled, then cocked her head. "You're not frightened of a little needle, are you? Big boy like you?" Sighing, he held out his arm and looked away, pulling a face as the point went in.

"There's a good chap . . . Okay, we're all set. You can pop these on now, and someone'll be along in a minute to take it from there."

He was handed what looked like a prisoner's outfit, grey tracksuit top and bottoms. "When do I get my own clothes back?" Peel asked.

"In due course."

"And my . . ." He tapped his eye socket. "Sentimental value."

Kingsley nodded. "I'll see to it. Promise." She patted him on the arm, and the next thing he knew she was gone—taking all her equipment with her. As Peel got dressed, two chairs were brought in and placed on either side of the table. Then a man with a military haircut entered. He was dressed all in black, wore octagonal glasses and held a clipboard in one hand—the other he held out for Peel to sit down. Then he put that same hand in his pocket and took out the missing eye-patch, tossing it onto the table.

"Compliments of the good doctor," he told Peel.

What followed over the next few hours was a grilling the likes of which he had never experienced, not even after the incident at the motel. Question after question . . . most of which he simply refused to answer (what the fuck did his childhood have to do with anything?). It went on for so long, he began to regret what he'd said to Pat about caution. These people took it to an art form!

Just when he thought it wouldn't end, and was beginning to get annoyed, especially with the interviewer's attitude ("Look mate, I haven't done a thing wrong—apart from stopping one of your people becoming a hot meal!") it was suddenly over and he was shown to a room with a bunk and a metal toilet in it. That did little to combat the whole prisoner thing, especially when the door was locked behind him again.

With nothing else to do, Peel lay back on the bed, arm behind his head. He didn't think he'd drop off, but hadn't realised quite how exhausted he was. Pat had been right after all, he did need sleep—and in somewhere he knew wouldn't be attacked anytime soon.

He woke when the door opened again, and standing there was another soldier he hadn't seen before. No guns this time, just an easy smile as the dark-skinned young man offered to show him where he could get some food.

"You'll probably be given the official tour another time," the lad said; couldn't have been that much older than Pat. "Did they put you through the wringer?"

"I've been through worse," Peel answered.

"They do it first time to all the new recruits."

"I'm not a recruit," Peel informed him.

"Yeah, well . . ." was the only reply. Then they were there, at the canteen. It looked like any other work canteen, at a factory, a hospital, but Peel still found himself sucking in a breath at the sight. More people than he'd seen in such a long time, all in one place. Chatting, eating, drinking. Most of them had military uniforms on, and those that didn't had white coats like Dr Kingsley. "Here we are. Just help yourself. Choice is pretty limited, though, I'm afraid." And by that the boy meant limited to tan-coloured slop, green-coloured slop, or yellow-coloured slop. When Pat had said get some decent food, she'd been exaggerating more than a little—but it was still better than what he'd been managing on out there of late. "If you need anything, just give us a shout. Name's Eddie," the boy finished and headed off.

That was when she'd found him again: Pat. He had a sneaking suspicion she'd been waiting here for him in fact, hanging around until they were satisfied he wasn't a threat. "So," she said, jamming more of her own meal into her mouth, "what do you reckon? Place is pretty good right? Was here even before everything went to pot."

"S'okay," Peel repeated. "Not mad keen on the way they treat their guests, I have to say."

"Sorry," Pat offered, possibly on behalf of the whole of 1A. "They're being extra careful at the moment, I think. Lot of stuff going on out there."

"Always has been," he reminded her, as if she needed it.

"I mean worse than usual. 7B wasn't the only place to be infiltrated recently. There have been others . . . It's like they're making a concerted effort to mop up the rest of us."

"They probably are." Peel took a sip of his drink.

"Lot of casualties. I heard a few survivors of 5C talking, they barely got out of that one alive. If it hadn't been for . . ." Pat shrugged. "It's why we need all the help we can get."

Peel held up his hand. "Whoa, whoa. Look, I'm not staying. A bed and something to eat, that's what you said."

"I know, but—"

"I'm just not a team player, sweetheart. Been doing this on my own far too long for that."

"Don't call me that," she snapped, slamming down her spoon.

"What?"

"Sweetheart." For a moment he thought it was the 'girl' thing again, then she added: "You're not my dad."

He shook his head. "I'm sorry, I didn't . . ." Peel closed his mouth; wasn't sure how to reply. Thinking about it, he'd definitely said the word in a way—in a tone—that felt very much like a parent talking to his child; something Pat had obviously picked up on too. It had just slipped out—but why? He'd chosen a life, or it had been chosen for him, where a family hadn't been possible. Peel wasn't going to put a wife or kids in danger like that. But hadn't there always been that longing inside him, even when he moved on to the next town or city, tracking target after target? He'd pushed it down, though, deeper than they were right now under those rocks. Once the apocalypse had hit, he'd thought it had been buried forever—then Pat had come along, and he'd saved her. And perhaps, just perhaps, something had been unearthed then, not to mention during the short time they'd spent together. The way she'd taken hold of his hand. She looked more sad than angry now, probably at the thought of him leaving more than anything. He decided to redirect the conversation. "What's with all this pretending to be something you're not anyway?"

"How do you mean?"

"Making out you're a bloke. There are women here, soldiers even. Your Colonel Alkins that you told me about . . . Why do you feel the need to hide who you are? *How* have you even hidden it? That Dr Kingsley is pretty thorough."

Pat looked down. "They . . . The squadron who found me just assumed, and I let them. Kept on letting them. The doc is the only other person here who knows and she promised to keep it to herself."

Yeah, she was pretty good with those promises, thought Peel. "But why? I still don't—"

"Because . . ." Pat looked around, lowered her voice. "Because it's just easier, is all. You're treated differently."

"Only if you let people. Some of the strongest folk I've ever known have been women. Mum, bless her soul. Single mother who held down a job and still brought me up. She took after my Nan."

"It's . . . it's not the same thing," argued Pat.

"Isn't it? It's all strength. You survived out there on your own all that time. Handled yourself well back there at 7B, too. That was pretty damned badass, if you ask me." He felt like adding, *if I was your dad I'd be proud of you.* "They should give you a bloody medal."

"Now you're making fun of me."

"Not at all," he said seriously.

There was a hint of a smile starting on her face when he said that, but then it was gone again. "We're . . . They . . . You just wouldn't understand."

"Try me," he said.

She opened her mouth to say something but seemed to get distracted. Peel followed her gaze, saw what she was gawking at. Another young lad, this one wearing a cap. There was something very familiar about him, but Peel couldn't quite put his finger on it. He walked past them, nodded to her, then continued on. Pat's eyes trailed him as he picked up a bowl and drink of his own. But then he left the room again, clearly wanting to be on his own.

"So," Peel said when she faced him. "How long?"

"Hmm?" Pat suddenly focused again. "What? How long what?"

"How long have you been in love with that guy?"

"I'm not . . . We're just . . . Tommy's not . . ." It was her turn to go red now.

Peel grinned. "Oh no, of course not. And, by the way, he knows."

"Knows about . . ." She was frowning, looking worried now.

"How you feel *and* the fact you're not a fella."

"*What?* How?" The redness had deepened considerably.

"Same way I knew, I guess. We're not morons. Question is, what are you going to do about it?"

Pat went quiet for a moment or two, digesting all this. They were still sitting in silence when another shadow fell across their table. Peel looked up again to see Dr Kingsley standing there. "Hi Pat."

"Doc."

"And *hello*, Peel. I've been looking for you, actually."

"You . . . you have?" he said.

"Yes." She left quite a gap before her next sentence. "Thought you'd like to know the bloods came back clean as a whistle." Peel nodded, gave her his thanks. "Okay, right . . ." She clapped her hands. "Well, I'll leave you two in peace then."

"Thanks doctor," Peel said again. When he looked back over at Pat, he saw her smirking. "What?"

"You can talk," she said.

CHAPTER THREE

SOMETHING JUST WASN'T RIGHT.

He could sense it, and if nothing else over the years he'd learned to trust those instincts. They'd got him out of any number of scrapes, even before the world had gone barking (ha!) mad.

Tommy kept on walking, along one corridor and down another. Descending steps, taking short hops in lifts. Going deeper and deeper into the base, into the maze that was 1A. It didn't have a back door, a way to get in from behind—which was how the wolves had breached 5C he was told—so eventually he'd reach his destination: the very lowest point in here. Unlike the more hastily-constructed warrens out there, this was a place that had been built a long time ago and kept secret, just in case everything in the outside world ended up in the toilet. He was willing to bet that nobody ever thought it would be because of *them*. Wars between men, sure. Plagues, of course. Never what actually happened.

Definitely not General Grice. He wouldn't have had the foresight to see something like this coming, to imagine a world overrun by those creatures—killing or turning every human being they could find until . . . That was the plan, anyway, but the mutts hadn't banked on the resilience of humankind. There might not be many of them left, but they fought. By God, how they fought! And they had a plan. An endgame.

All of which might be in jeopardy right now, because something was really, really wrong. He could feel it. Not that Grice would listen.

"Look, I know what they all think of you out there. I know what they're saying, how they reckon you're the fucking second coming or something! But to me you're just another grunt. And a wet behind the ears one at that!"

Yeah, a wet behind the ears grunt who'd just saved what was left of the base at 5C—admittedly, not that many men, but even so . . . Had somehow known they were in trouble, and saved them by leading all those bastards away through that wrecked park. So many chasing him, and they were so fast. Even after he'd tossed back a couple of silver frag grenades, it was inevitable that they'd catch up. In spite of the fact he'd dodged left and right, avoiding them as they raced up behind him, one had clipped the back of his bike and sent it spinning out of control.

Tommy was lucky to have landed how he did, because he could have been seriously injured. Though that was the least of his problems he found, when he clambered to his feet and saw that tidal wave of fur in front of him, still heading in his direction. Only to stop right at the last moment, when he thought he was a dead man. Stop and just stare at him as he was slowly rising. What were they fucking waiting for? To see if he'd lob another grenade?

Don't question it, he told himself: just get out of there. Tommy had inched sideways to the bike, all those red eyes watching him. Had righted it and hopped back on, setting off again. He'd risked one last look over his shoulder, but the wolves were still standing there, not giving chase at all. Head down, Tommy had slipped through the gap in the broken railings at the back of the park, then sped up again on the open streets. He'd returned to 1A the long way round, just in case he was being trailed—was that it, had that been why they'd let him go? —gone through the security checks, which thankfully hadn't been as stringent as when he'd first arrived, before catching up with Ridgeway and his men who'd been back some time.

"There's someone here who'd like to say thanks," Ridgeway had told him, introducing Tommy to one of the blokes they'd got out of that bus. "Told you he'd be fine, didn't I?"

The man, who was called Angel apparently—and Ridgeway had joked that you didn't see many of those around here—had nodded. Had hardly been able to get his words of gratitude out. At one point Tommy thought he was going to bow or something.

How they think you're the fucking second coming!

He wasn't anything like that, he was just lucky. Luckier than most, especially that night. And he'd learnt to trust his instincts, just like Grice should be doing right now. Because something just wasn't right. That man could be such a prick sometimes, couldn't see past the end of his nose, which admittedly wasn't so easy when it was as big as his. But his words, his refusal to acknowledge what he called Tommy's 'stupid bloody hunches' had made him doubt himself on more than one occasion—only to be proven right in the end.

And reporting in, being debriefed, had got him doubting himself again . . . Hadn't it? He *knew* something wasn't right, that something was in the air. Yet he was still heading down and down, wasn't he? Needed to confirm it with the only other source he really trusted. *Used to* trust at any rate. Maybe that was one of the reasons he hadn't visited lately. Not since the last time, since—

It was high time he did though, he realised that. He'd needed to make a pit-stop first, grab food and drink from the canteen. Pat had been there, and he was genuinely pleased to see her; should probably have stopped and said hello or something. But she was with the guy who by all accounts had saved her from that mess at 7B, or the aftermath of it. And Tommy was too distracted anyway, didn't really feel like talking today as they usually did, explaining where he was going or why. So he'd just gone off again once he'd loaded himself up.

Unlike the others that had been in there, he wouldn't be eating it himself; wasn't all that hungry actually. That was why he still had the bowl and drink in his hands as he continued on through the base. It was still early enough that the first of the twice daily deliveries of sustenance wouldn't have been left yet. There were less than a handful of people he trusted to do that—Ridgeway included. People who owed him their lives, and even they didn't know why they were doing it. Understood someone special was inside the room (they didn't know the half of it), but they were always told to just leave the food and drink outside the door. Tommy knew some of those trusted folk speculated there was a defector inside. Someone who'd been turned back and had vital information about the war effort. Or maybe it was a VIP, a high-ranking official of some kind.

None of them knew for sure. Their commanding officer didn't even know the place existed, because he'd taken over after the person who let them in had died. Had killed himself, slit his wrists rather than go on leading a resistance he thought was doomed. Nicholson his name had been, Tommy recalled. Only a few years ago, but it seemed like decades. Sometimes Tommy wondered if that man hadn't done the right thing; at least he was at peace now while they all carried on struggling against an enemy which showed no signs of weakening.

But that was no way to think. It was shit like that which lost wars, and more than anything else Tommy hated losing at anything; always had.

He got it from her.

But as the lift doors opened and he looked up that final corridor into the deepest part of this whole glorified underground bunker, the nerves kicked in again. He had no idea what he'd find, whether it would be a good day or bad one (was there even such a thing as a good day anymore?). Or a *really* bad one. But the love was there, the sense of loyalty that only came from going through what they had together. Loyalty beyond family ties, greater than just the normal bond most people like them shared.

Tommy realised he'd paused. That his legs were no longer carrying him forwards. He swallowed dryly. This had been a bad idea—such a bad idea. But now he was here, he needed to just get on with it. He owed her so much, couldn't even begin to repay any of that. Owed her his time now, regardless of everything.

He took a step. Then another, and another, his pulse getting quicker with each one.

Tommy reached the door much faster than he'd anticipated, than he was happy with. There was an empty bowl and cup on the floor outside it, left there from the last meal. Tommy knew it would be locked from the inside, always was. He thought about knocking, but nine times out of ten you wouldn't even get a response that way. He'd once waited out here fifteen minutes, knocking and calling out periodically. In the end he'd always done what he was about to do right now, which was use the key-card he had in his pocket to gain admittance. Transferring the bowl and cup to one hand, he was about to shove this into the slot and slide it downwards when he noticed from this angle the door was actually open a crack.

Tommy put the card away, frowning. Then he swallowed again, reached out to push the door open. His fingers brushed the surface, as if he might be able to sense what he'd find inside first—which was pure nonsense. There was only one way to find that out, and so he shoved it, a little harder than was strictly necessary.

It was dim in there, and as he stepped through he needed a moment or two for his eyes to adjust. Something moved off to the side of him and he jumped, turning as something else did the same on the other side of him. If his heart hadn't been racing before, it certainly was now.

Then he realised that the people, the faces greeting him were doing exactly the same as he was, mirroring his actions. There was a reason for that, because what he was looking at *were* mirrors. But those weren't the only ones, far from it. As Tommy looked up and around him, he saw dozens and dozens of the things; all hanging from the walls, stuck to the ceiling, leaving not a scrap of either visible in fact. He knew this, but always seemed to forget. She'd been insistent on 'decorating' this room herself when she retreated down here, finding as many as she could, getting him to find others out there—and Tommy often wondered if that had been a terrible mistake. It had seemed to calm her down at first, offering protection in a place already fortified (a place she had directed them both to), but now it just made her more agitated than ever.

There was a terrible scream, so loud it deafened him for a second or so. Tommy reeled, then stepped backwards when he realised that out of the darkness a figure with long, matted hair was lunging at him. He dropped the bowl and cup, almost slipping because of the spillage—but it did allow him to grab this person by the arms. Stop her from doing any damage with those nails of hers, which grew at an extraordinary rate regardless of how many times they were cut.

Not one to be deterred, the person attempted to bite him instead. Teeth snapping, cracking together as the mouth opened, then closed, again and again. It was all Tommy could do to keep her away from his face and neck. Trying not to hurt her, he shoved her back, letting go in the process. She came at him once more, still all claws and teeth and mad hair. Again he threw her back, this time to land on a chair that was in the centre of the room. The mirrors all around her reflected the action a million times. The chair wobbled, and for a moment Tommy thought she was going to tip over backwards on it, but then it righted itself.

She looked like she was about to rise and come at him again, but he held up his hand; a gesture of placation he thought. He *hoped.*

"Stay down. *Please.*" She frowned at him, eyebrows knitting together. "Stop Mum. Just stop. It's me . . . It's Tommy. It's *your* Tommy."

The woman squinted now, but remained where she was. The respite allowed him to take her in for the first time and she'd aged even in the short while since he'd last been here. She was only in her forties, but looked sixty or seventy. It had been a hard life Tommy knew, even before all this, but would that put decades on you? His mother looked ancient, actually. Like Miss Havisham waiting in the attic. Waiting for his father, maybe, who they both knew would never come.

She made a sudden move and he took up a defensive stance; couldn't help it, that was just his training kicking in. But she wasn't about to attack again, just reaching down and grabbing something from the floor. A wooden box which she now cradled, as she very often did. Tommy knew what was inside it, she'd shown him once—though these days she always kept it locked, the key around her neck. Keep-sakes from the old days: photos of friends, family; trinkets, from before he was born and after, when they'd moved from place to place, never with any explanation . . . none that made any sense anyway. Keeping below the radar, assuming false identities and his mum working cash in hand so they could get by, as well as teaching him at home (not that they ever had a real home) because she couldn't risk Tommy going to school.

"Mum?" he tried again. "Mum, are . . . are you okay?" A stupid question, and he regretted it as soon as it was out of his mouth. She was quite clearly not okay, had gotten worse since he'd seen her last. "It's Tommy."

She shook her head at that. "You're not little Tommy," she replied. It was the first time he'd heard her voice in ages, and the croaky nature of it was almost as shocking as what she was saying. Maybe the scream had caused that?

Tommy rubbed his face. Not this again. "It is me, honest."

No reply.

"I brought you something to eat, to drink," he told her, then remembered what had happened to it. Looked down at the mess on the floor he'd have to clean up before he left again so she wouldn't hurt herself. "I really wish you'd let Dr Kingsley take a look at you, there might be something she could—"

"No doctors!" she shouted, her voice growing stronger.

"All right, all right—whatever you say, Mum. No worries." Tommy edged a bit closer, ready to defend himself if anything happened, although she looked to be calming down a bit. He'd probably just scared her. "I . . . I came here because I need your help, Mum."

She was staring down at the box, didn't even seem to be listening to him.

"Mum, *please*. I don't know who else to go to with this. I really need you to focus." Yeah, right. Like that was going to happen.

The woman did look up again, though, studying his face. "You . . . you look so much like him, you know," she said then.

"Who, Dad?" Tommy had never known his father, the man had died before he came along, but his mum had told him stories about the man. About how he fought those things out there before anyone really knew about them. That he'd been a hero. That they'd only been together a short space of time, but loved each other so very much. That it was one of those fuckers who'd killed him while he was trying to protect her, while Tommy was still in her womb.

She nodded. "Same smile, same eyes." He thought she was going to start crying, as she often did when she spoke about his father. But instead she laughed. "Denim on denim," the woman said.

"I-I don't know what that means, Mum." He shook his head. "I don't have time for this, I need to—"

"Time!" she shouted. "It's about time!" Then she nodded as if she'd just said the sagest thing in the world. "That's what your gran said to me . . . No, not to me . . . I thought it was me, but it wasn't. It was . . . She said that just before she was killed."

"Gran?" Now there was a woman his mum barely spoke about, if ever. Tommy got the impression it was too hard for her. All he knew about his mother's mother was that she was a strong woman as well. That they were both stronger than he would ever be. "She was killed? You've never told me that before. How . . . how did she die?" Tommy knew he should stay on point—his mum could go off into one again without warning—but now her name had been mentioned he found he needed to know.

"She was killed by . . . someone wearing my face."

One of them, then. A shapeshifter. His father *and* his gran? No wonder there was little love for those things in his family, aside from the obvious fact that they'd slaughtered countless people without mercy. Those two murders were what had made all so this personal.

"I . . . she came to see me, to make sure I was . . ." His mother looked him squarely in the eyes. "It's my fault. This whole thing is . . . If I'd just remembered to give Tilly . . ." She paused, looking down and to the left, then started mumbling, counting on her fingers by touching them with her thumb. "One: ring Mum . . . Can't now, she's gone. Two: do some tidying . . . Nothing to tidy, only the world. Three: ring Steph . . . Where is Steph, anyway? I miss her." Tommy knew who both of those people were, had seen photos of them: best friend, Steph, and the elderly lady his mother had once cared for, Tilly. But why was any of that important now? "Four: buy yourself a treat . . . Something to eat. Five, mend a broken . . . a broken heart. I—"

"Mum, stay with me. I need you to . . ." He sighed, this was going nowhere.

"I'm sorry," she told him, looking over again. "I shouldn't have put you in such . . . You shouldn't even be here, it's not possible. You shouldn't even *exist*. Neither of us should!"

She was talking about his birth now, his traumatic birth in a hotel room. By rights he shouldn't have survived, and neither should she. Maybe the sixth sense he had, his awareness, was down to that birth; certainly his spirit, the fight in him, was. No, his Mum had always known things—ever since he could remember. And especially about *them*. That's where he'd got it from, passed on. Tommy wondered absently if his gran or dad possessed similar gifts. Maybe that's what had made them so dangerous, and the reason they'd had to die?

"I know, Mum," he said. "I know."

"Shouldn't exist. Impossible." She shook her head. "And now we're paying the price. We're all paying the . . . Tommy, sweetheart."

"Yes, Mum. It's me."

His mother got up, placed the box on her chair and walked towards him. There was no maliciousness there now, just love. His hands were still out and she took them in hers. "This path we're on, Tommy—it'll be the death of both of us."

"No, Mum, don't say that."

"It's true. I've seen it. They're coming. *He's* coming, and I'm not sure I can . . . I'm so tired. Of fighting, of running."

"You don't have to run anymore, Mum. That was in the past."

She squeezed his hands so tightly. "Past, present and . . . future. All the same, all the same."

"I don't know what you're trying to tell me. Look, I came here because I got a sense that something was wrong out there."

"Something's wrong, something's wrong," she repeated, in a way that sounded a little like she was making fun of him. "Something's wrong all right. In here." Taking a hand away, she tapped her temple. "I'm losing my grip, Tommy. He's . . . I can't hold him at bay. Can't hold any of them!"

She was losing her grip definitely, didn't take Dr Kingsley to see that.

"They're coming. There'll be so much death."

"Who? The wolves? They don't know where we are, and they can't get in. You're safe, Mum. Trust me."

"None of us are *safe!* " she bellowed, then calmed down almost immediately. "This . . . this whatever it is." She tapped her head again. "I get it from him. *You* get it from him."

"From Dad?" Tommy was struggling to make sense of all this, it was more incoherent than usual.

"No, no, no. From *Him!* " She nodded to the side and Tommy looked. For a fraction of a second, he could have sworn he saw something there. Something in his mother's reflection. Something that was her, but wasn't her.

Something with glowing red eyes.

He blinked and the image was gone. She was back again, looking down and letting out a slow, weary breath. "You have to do something," was all she would say after that. "I can't. But maybe *you* could."

"What Mum? What do I need to do?" His hands were on the outside of hers now, he was the one doing the squeezing.

She suddenly broke free, whirling and returning to the chair—snatching up the box and cradling it like the baby she'd thought he was when he came in. Little Tommy. He stepped forward, hand reaching out, but he was losing her again. There was more mumbling, but he couldn't make out the words. In the end he gave up, cleaned up the mess from before as best he could, and told her he'd arrange for someone else to bring a meal.

Then, just as he was leaving, he heard her say quietly: "I love you, Tommy."

He turned back, open-mouthed. It had been quite a while since she'd said that to him. "I . . . I love you too, Mum."

"Now go, go." Her face was contorted again, and she spat out the last word: "*Go!* "

Tommy made his way out through the door, shutting it, locking it so that only he could get inside.

"I love you," he said again, though she couldn't hear him now. Then he began to walk back up the corridor, leaving her behind. His mum.

The woman who had once been Rachael Daniels.

CHAPTER FOUR

SHE HAD A BAD FEELING. A FEELING THE MEETING HADN'T GONE well.

He'd warned her not to get her hopes up beforehand, had basically said that he'd be leaving soon—probably within the next day or so. And Pat could see that this place made Peel antsy, probably associated it with those people who'd cost him his job when he was younger. All the questioning, the palaver when he first arrived, hadn't helped with that. The mirrors in the lift should have been enough, a blood test or whatever. None of what they'd done had made him feel welcome or at home.

Except maybe meeting Dr Kingsley. She could tell he liked her . . . a lot. That it was mutual—the doc rarely bothered with the personal touch.

Question is, what are you going to do about it?

His words to her about Tommy, which she could have repeated to him. Perhaps to get him to stay, for a little while longer at least. There'd barely been enough time to get to know each other properly, to hang out. Pat wasn't entirely sure why she wanted that, just knew she did. Knew there was some kind of bond which they could both feel. And that crack about him not being her dad . . . Yes, it was exactly how her father had talked to her, what he'd called her—and it reminded her in that instant of the gaping loss she still felt. But it was also reminding her that this man who'd saved her would be gone soon as well, that she'd probably never see him again. Pat wasn't sure she would be able to bear that.

Maybe if the doc and Peel got together not only would he stay, but they could be . . . What? Some kind of crazy makeshift family, to replace the one that she'd lost? Pat shook her head. It was insane, stupid to think about such things especially the way the world was now. New bonds, new families were formed—she'd seen it—but they were also torn apart again in a heartbeat. More misery, more loss. Could she take that again?

Wouldn't it be better to let Peel go? Wouldn't being part of that family, the loving daughter, change how she was treated around here? How people looked at her, how they were with her? It was what she'd been trying to explain to Peel when he asked about the 'pretending to be something she wasn't'. Of course she knew there were strong women here, and out there as well. The doc for one, Alkins before she'd . . . That wasn't the issue. They were older, and had fought tooth and nail to get that respect; Pat wasn't sure she was tough enough to do that. More often than not, women were still pushed off to the sidelines, relegated to jobs like childcare—and reminded that the future, if humanity even had one, depended on them. That without them there would be no repopulation. The same old story . . .

Was she being a traitor to her sex though by not standing up to be counted? Probably. Almost definitely. She'd proved her worth by now, and all Peel's talk about strong women had got her thinking. Perhaps it *was* time to stop pretending, to stop hiding? According to Peel most people, including Tommy, realised it anyway—and didn't care. If she just came right out with it, would she be inspiring others to follow her lead, to eventually become someone to look up to like Alkins? Like Peel's mum and his nan? The way he'd talked about them, with such pride. Such admiration.

Back to Peel again, and what he might do. How that meeting might have gone. General Grice had personally requested to see 'the newbie' as he called him—in spite of the fact there was only about a decade between the two men and in terms of experience, Peel probably even had the edge on him. She knew he'd be trying to get him to stay too, join the cause instead of being out there on his own running rogue. God, he could do so much good here if he did; the way he fought . . . It reminded her of Tommy, actually. Where he had youth on his side, Peel more than made up for that with skill and experience. Together, they could probably take on the wolves alone and come out on top. Could certainly do their fair share of inspiring others, if nothing else.

But one thing Peel had shown he couldn't do was toe the line, follow orders, especially if he disagreed with them. He'd been a loner all this time, made his own decisions; all things that would have been reported back after his evaluation. Grice wasn't the friendliest of people at the best of times, persuasion not one of his strong suits, so it was unlikely he'd give an inch. Just look at how he rubbed Tommy up the wrong way all the time, refused to listen just because of how young he was.

So, when she'd headed off to catch up with Peel—to track *him* down after the meeting with Grice and see how things had gone— she wasn't surprised to see the man standing in the corridor with a serious expression on his face, rubbing his bearded chin. What she *was* surprised to see was Tommy standing with him, talking to him, sporting an equally grave expression.

She almost turned back again, but something made her continue on. Curiosity, not just to find out how the head-to-head with Grice had gone, but also now to see what those two could possibly be talking about. Her?

What are you going to do about it?

Was Peel saying something to Tommy about how she felt, a parting gift that could actually ruin everything? Ruin their friendship (although why hadn't he stopped to talk to her in the canteen? that was still smarting).

Get over yourself, Pat thought. *Not everything revolves around you.* Besides, Peel didn't strike her as someone who would get in the middle of all that; he wouldn't view it as his business. A private chat between him and her, that was one thing—but Peel didn't know Tommy. *Hadn't* known him, though they seemed pretty chummy right at that moment. So chummy in fact she almost turned around again, if they hadn't spotted her at that moment.

And was there a look on Tommy's face then that said he wished she wasn't there, that she hadn't interrupted them? A look that said he was anything but happy to see her? A look actually mirrored by Peel, now he saw her as well. Pointed looks that did nothing to help with that confidence she might have been feeling, the strength inside.

Pat raised her hand a little in greeting. Tommy nodded again, just as he had done back at the canteen. Like they hardly knew each other. Like he was trying to keep her at a distance? *Because* he knew how she felt, as Peel had said?

"Hi there," said Peel. No sweetheart now, no comforting words of wisdom. "You okay?"

"Are you?" she asked, then looked from him to Tommy and back again—still no clue as to what this was about.

Peel sighed. "Depends on how you look at it. Seems like I might be leaving even sooner than I thought, kid."

Pat scowled. "I'm not—"

He raised his own hand, more sharply than she had. "A kid. Right, I know the routine by now. Just a figure of speech."

She glanced at Tommy again; it was mainly because of him that she'd reacted this time. Didn't want him thinking of her as a kid, a girl . . . Or did she? Maybe girl was all right. She'd be okay with girl. Kinda. Pat remembered what they'd been talking about, Peel going away. "Why? Was it something from the meeting, something Grice said?"

"Oh, that prick! Couldn't find his arse with both hands and someone holding up a mirror."

"Agreed," said Tommy, speaking for the first time since she'd arrived.

"How on earth did that twat get to be the boss of *anything*, let alone the whole shebang?"

"By default," Tommy informed Peel.

"Jesus, you'd make a better leader than that maggot!"

"That's what I keep telling him," said Pat, desperate to be part of the conversation. A conversation that had gotten off track again. That had frozen up when she came along.

"And it's like I keep saying, I don't want that kind of responsibility," replied Tommy.

"They'd follow you," she argued. "We . . . we all would."

"That's not the point." There was something in his tone; he was pissed off. Might not even have been at her, but the last thing she wanted today was a row with Tommy. "Look, let's just forget about it. Grice's in charge and that's that."

"So you're leaving because of that, because you don't get on?" She directed her question at Peel now, giving Tommy a chance to cool down.

"Not just because of that. I told you before—"

"You're just not a team player, right?" Pat said, interrupting him this time. "Didn't look that way to me, you two seemed as thick as thieves before I came along."

The two men exchanged furtive glances, and it was Tommy who spoke up first. "I just wanted to say hello to our visitor . . . Before he left."

"*R-i-ght,*" said Pat, looking as him sideways on. "Tommy, I know you've been doing a good impression of someone who's never come across me in his life, but I actually know you better than that. I know when you're lying for a start."

Tommy couldn't hold her gaze; those blue eyes pointing down, to the left, anywhere but at Pat.

"What's going on?" She was back on Peel again, because Tommy was saying nothing.

He sighed once more. "Look, your man here . . ."

"He's not . . ." Pat let the sentence tail off.

Tommy finally raised his head, but it was more of a warning than about what had been said: "Peel . . ."

"She's going to find out eventually, you do realise that. I've only known her a couple of days and I get that. He needs a tracker," Peel informed her.

"Now you've done it," said Tommy, taking off his cap and running a hand through his tousled hair before replacing it again.

"Why do you need a . . . Is this some kind of mission?" Pat almost jumped up and down on the spot.

Tommy put a finger to his lips. "Not so loud, Pat!"

She lowered her voice. "It's a *secret* mission?"

Peel laughed. "It's so secret not even Grice knows about it."

"What?" Her head was swimming.

"It's off the books," Tommy said to her. "Grice would never agree to it."

"Which is why I'm on the verge of saying yes," Peel added.

"A tracker . . ." Pat repeated.

"A hunter," stated Tommy. "I need someone who *thinks* like they do."

"Takes a bastard to catch a bastard, right?" Peel was puffing out his chest like he was proud of the fact.

"Something like that."

Pat let out a breath. "You want to *catch* one of those things? Are you crazy?" She'd never heard of anyone even attempting such a thing. Damned right Grice wouldn't greenlight something like that. You killed mutts, preferably before they killed you. "Why ever would you want one?"

"Doesn't matter, I just do," said Tommy. "So, are we cool here?"

"Cool?" Pat thought about that for a moment. "That depends . . . Are you going with him?"

Tommy bit his lip, clearly thinking about the best way to answer. In the end he told her the truth. "*I* am. But *you're* definitely not. See? I do know you."

"But . . . I could help."

"Pat, you need to listen to him. This doesn't involve you."

It was Tommy's turn finally to put up his hand; in fact he put up both of them. And he was shaking his head, because he knew that was absolutely the wrong thing to say to her. Deep down, Pat understood that they were both trying to keep her out of the frame in case it went sour. Plausible deniability, they called it—she'd heard it used before. Heard Tommy use it actually. Or, they might just be trying to keep her safe—and the fact that both of them, Tommy especially, thought that much of her did make her feel a little better. But basically flat-out telling her she *couldn't* be involved in their little secret mission . . . Tommy was right, it was guaranteed to put her back up. Guaranteed to make her say what she said next.

"I could always go and tell Grice."

Both of them looked at her in a different way now, gaping in disbelief. "You wouldn't," said Tommy.

Pat shrugged.

"And you say you're not a kid, going off to tell the headmaster on us." Peel folded his arms and shook his head.

"I don't *want* to. I just want to help. Tag along. I won't be any trouble, I promise."

"A minute ago you were calling us crazy," Tommy reminded her. "Now you want to go with us?"

"I-I just want to help," she repeated. "You remember what you were saying about your mum, your nan?" Peel nodded reluctantly, understanding what she was driving at, while Tommy just looked confused.

"Okay," said Peel eventually, unfolding his arms, "you can come along."

"Hey, my mission," argued Tommy.

"But you *need* me."

Tommy threw back his head. "All right, all right. But we'd better get a move on if we're going to do this."

"Yep," said Peel. "And you'd better get me my stuff back—including my hat and my axe."

Tommy nodded. "Not a problem. Meet you back here in half an hour?" He gave Pat one last, quick look, then headed off.

"Well, when I asked what you were going to do about . . . y'know . . . blackmail wasn't quite what I had in mind," said Peel.

Pat groaned. "He'll get over it . . . hopefully. I'd rather be out there with him—with both of you—than sat here on my own worrying. Now that I know what you're up to."

"You sure about that? This isn't going to be no picnic."

"Never is out there," Pat answered, a little too quickly. A little too defensively.

"Catching one is going to be very different to avoiding them, carrying your messages from place to place."

"I know," she said, sounding exactly like the teenager she was. "I can help."

"Yeah," said Peel. "That's exactly what I'm afraid of."

Pat didn't have a clue what he meant by that and before she could ask him, he'd wandered off as well.

Leaving her standing there in the corridor alone, the bad feeling she'd had on her way here returning with interest.

CHAPTER FIVE

H E WAS WILLING TO BET PAT HADN'T HAD THIS IN MIND WHEN SHE strong-armed them into letting her come along.

Peel raised the binoculars again, focussing on the girl—woman— out there on the street. On the floor, crying out, left leg covered in blood. He gritted his teeth, ground them at the back, feeling more helpless than he ever had in his life. Body twitching, almost springing up and going to her more than once.

That's what happens when you actually start to care *about people,* he reminded himself. *It's why you never have before.*

What was he supposed to do then, just let the wolves savage her back there when she was running from them? No, he never would have let that happen (wasn't that what was happening now?). But he shouldn't have let her come along, back then or now. Shouldn't have let her talk him into going back with her to 1A either; he hadn't been that desperate for a bed or meal.

Admit it, you wanted *to go back with her. You were starting to get attached even then.*

It was why he'd been so keen to leave again, once he could see she was safe. Why bringing her out here on this stupid mission her boyfriend had cooked up was the worst idea in the history of bad ideas. Putting himself in harm's way was one thing, he was used to that, but he'd known at some point Pat would be in danger as well—and that was something completely different. Something completely new to him, alien even.

He looked over to his left, at said boyfriend. Well, friend anyway. He was just as twitchy, just as tense. Sweat was pouring from under that cap of his as he stared out at the scene. You couldn't mistake it; he cared about Pat, too. More than cared. They needed putting in a bag and shaking up, as his old mum used to say. Dancing around it, when it was obvious her feelings for him were reciprocated big time. It's why he'd been so off with her when she'd pressured them back in the corridor. Hated she was out here just as much as Peel did, though neither of them could do a thing about it.

Just like they couldn't do a thing about her being on the ground there, wounded, tears rolling down her cheeks and screaming for help.

He ground his teeth again, probably not a good thing to do in a post-apocalyptic world where there were no dentists. Although they'd almost certainly have one back at 1A; they had everything frigging else! Perhaps Dr Kingsley handled that side of things, along with all the other medical stuff? And he allowed himself a moment to picture that woman's face, her smile.

Who was dancing around who again?

There were more important things to think about right at that minute, like Pat out there. They were both watching her, both unable to do a thing. Same as the man across the way, their other companion on this fool's errand. Tommy had kept that quiet until they arrived at the vehicles, and he'd actually been there waiting for them. Nobody ever asked about his comings and goings apparently, while Tommy had to say that he and Pat were escorting Peel from the base after he'd declined to remain there. Word had probably spread about that now, as well, and absently he wondered if the 'good doctor' had heard? What she thought about him leaving . . . Not that he actually was, not yet anyway. He was still attached to that place, in more ways than one.

Once Tommy had given Peel back his things, they'd travelled up to the surface in the lift, then headed off in the direction of the vehicles—which were camouflaged and hidden nearby. Or at least theirs were: a battered old estate that could pass for a wreck when they needed to park up and go on foot; and Tommy's faithful motorbike. He'd scope up ahead on that, he explained, making sure the way was clear for the rest of them . . .

Including him. The newest member of the team, who'd been standing there leaning on the car and waiting for the others to arrive.

"I believe you've met Mr Waterhouse," said Tommy, holding out his hand by way of an introduction.

In front of them was the man wearing octagonal glasses, dressed all in black, who'd questioned Peel extensively—and in his view unnecessarily—after his medical. "My interrogator," he'd said in response. "I didn't realise we'd be bringing along another sightseer." Pat's face had scrunched up again at that remark.

"We aren't. Mr Waterhouse is here for a reason. When you've done your job, he'll do his."

"And that was hardly an interrogation, Mr Peel," said the man himself finally, with a chilling grin.

"Mr Waterhouse has a certain set of skills," Tommy clarified, smiling as well.

"Runs in my family," added Waterhouse.

"Plus he owes me a favour or two."

There was no point discussing it further, this was Tommy's shout after all. Which was when he'd turned and asked Peel about the best way forward, what he had in mind.

"Okay, so you're talking about a two part operation. First the tracking . . . You're never going to find one of those things on its own, not nowadays. They run in packs, as you probably know. The trick is to find a pack that's not got that many members. There are some, I know the general areas they hang out. Second part is the catching. You want one alive, which is not going to be easy."

"Mr Waterhouse, do you have the tranq gun I asked you to bring along?"

"Already in the back of the car," the man told Tommy.

"All right," continued Peel. "That'll subdue one, assuming you have tranqs strong enough to put the bugger under." Waterhouse gave a nod. "But you still need to catch it first, contain it so you can get a decent shot in. Pit traps, you'd probably snag more than one with those. Snares? You'd have to get it in the right place at the right time. Not easy. Then there's the matter of bait." He stopped, as they looked at him and each other in turn. "Good hunter lures his prey to where they want them, then *bam!*" He'd made them jump by smacking his fist into the palm of his hand. "You got anything that they might want? Something they can't resist?" They'd looked at him blankly once more. "Bloody good razor, giant toothbrush? That kind of thing?"

"There's something they always want," Tommy had said at that point, then touched his chest with his thumb. And it was true, those creatures were always thirsty for more human flesh. Those they didn't turn, they ate, washing it all down with the blood of their victims.

"*No!*" Pat had virtually screamed out the word, knowing what Tommy meant. Realising that he was practically offering himself up as that bait. Peel had to admit, she was right. That wasn't what he'd had in mind at all, it was way too risky to put someone out there to draw in those fuckers. The capacity for something to go wrong was huge, like not being able to get out of the way in time before they pounced, getting caught in the subsequent crossfire. But then she surprised them all again, by saying: "Me! It should be me. I'll do it."

"*What?*" Tommy's pitch had almost matched hers. "No way."

"Think about it, they can smell fear. They prefer it when people are vulnerable—and that's really not you, Tommy." She pointed at Waterhouse and Peel, just to cover herself. "It's not *any* of you. I can do vulnerable, sell it to them. I-I hate to actually say it out loud, but I'm the weakest here."

Peel had placed a hand on her shoulder. "Maybe physically, but what you just offered to do . . . I reckon that makes you the strongest and the bravest of us all. Even given all that, obviously it's out of the question."

Again, the wrong thing to say to her—or said in the wrong way. He'd meant that *nobody* should be doing it. Pat had shrugged off his hand. She was so stubborn . . . Tell her that she couldn't . . . shouldn't do something and it just made her all the more determined. By the time she was finished, they'd more or less *had* to agree; anything else made it sound like a slight on her capability. And in spite of everything, it was the one plan which had the greatest chance of success, he had to admit that.

So, off they set. Tommy out in front on the bike as he said, finding them safe passage to the area Peel had suggested—or as near as dammit as they could get with the vehicles before having to creep up to it on foot. Waterhouse had insisted on driving the car, which actually Peel had no problem with. It had been so long since he'd driven himself he wasn't even sure he still could; didn't want to test that here and now, or after starting up an argument with the man in glasses.

Hardly anyone spoke on the journey. Their driver was concentrating on the road, guiding the car slowly and carefully towards the city, following Tommy up ahead. Pat was probably still mad with Peel, that was the sulky vibe she was giving off. While he was sitting there worrying about what would happen to her, going over all the scenarios in his head and not one of them ending well.

When they eventually parked, so that Peel could try and pick up a trail, Pat had hung back with Tommy and Waterhouse. More than once, instead of concentrating on what he should be doing, Peel had been thinking about a different journey on a different day. They'd talked then, got to know each other a bit—and he wished he'd had more of a chance to do that now. Before she offered herself up to those damned hounds like some kind of sacrifice of old. Before she went and got herself killed . . .

Coming across their tracks, a party of about half a dozen, he'd brought them abruptly to a halt. But it had also taken his mind off what would happen when they caught up to the pack.

Before they did, and before they set up their trap, Waterhouse had sprayed the three men with a masking scent to cover the fact they were there. "Something new we've developed," he explained. "We don't want them thinking about anything but our bait." He'd also suggested that they cut Pat. "Fresh blood will bring them here faster than anything." Which was true enough, but none of them wanted to hear it. Waterhouse also knew exactly where to do it so that there would be enough blood-loss, but no permanent damage. Pat had swallowed hard at that thought, everything suddenly becoming real for her.

"When it happens, we'll have to subdue them quickly," Peel had said as well. "They're unlikely to use that telepathic shit until they feel threatened. Less of the meal to share with others."

Another swallow.

It hadn't stopped her from going through with all this, however, and he had to admire her for that. Felt pride again, but hadn't felt able to tell her—though he wished to high Heaven, crouching down here now, that he had while he still could. Wasn't acting, either, he could see that. The fear was real, and coming off her in waves. They'd probably have found her even without the screams, the crying, but Pat was seeing this through and doing her best as usual.

She'd offered to help; now she was. And he recalled what he'd said back then, that he was worried about what that meant. Well, it had meant something like this. Watching her out there, waiting for those mutts to double back and come for her.

More than anything, he wanted to go and just grab her—run with her back to the relative safety of cover. Make sure she was safe, not exposed like she was now. Vulnerable, as she'd said herself.

I can do vulnerable, sell it to them.

Nothing to sell, it was all pretty genuine; would be for anyone. Especially now, especially as *they* were coming, creeping around the corner of a building—or what was left of that building at any rate—sniffing the air. Those crimson eyes blazing. All bristling with fur, mouths slavering as those long pink tongues unfurled, licking lips and running them over teeth that could bite a girder in half.

Pat stopped screaming suddenly. Stopped crying. Shock taking over. Looking like she either wanted to flee, or make an attempt at fending them off. The last time she'd seen their faces she'd had a chance . . . more or less. Now she was voluntarily laying there, bleeding, with no weapons at all, and she was torn.

She started screaming once again. Started crying again. The whole thing more real than ever. Her need desperate.

Peel was starting to get up, when Tommy's hand was suddenly on his arm. Not yet. He knew that already, same as the lad beside him, though all he really wanted to do was get Pat the fuck out of there.

Not yet—they weren't close enough yet. Nowhere near. 'Course, by the time they were it would be too late. Too late for them to reach her, too late for Pat.

They were coming, on and on. Coming for her.

Coming to kill her.

❧

They were coming.

Didn't matter how much she ran, whether she hid or stood and fought—*tried* to fight. Oh, but she was so, so tired. Tired of the struggle, of hiding away, of everything. Maybe it would be better if she just gave up? Just let them come. At least she'd get to see him again. Properly see him, not just in a reflection on her son's face. The man she loved. The man who'd been murdered so long ago.

No! He wouldn't have wanted her to give up. She *couldn't* give up, there was simply too much at stake. And yet—

It didn't matter if she was in the woods, in the cabin, on the estate—or in the cave. The original cave, or this cave . . . the one with the fake entrance that wasn't really an entrance (hadn't been hard to find; not for her).

They were coming whatever she did, wherever she went. Could smell her, smell her *blood* as it pumped through her veins. Wanted to shed it. Wanted to taste her, to eat her all up. Just like before.

Wanted to free something she'd kept locked away for a long time. Something that, if it was to get out, would spell the end of everything. They were losing, that much she knew. But when that happened, it would all be lost forever.

She'd buried it, so deep she didn't think anyone would ever be able to find it. So deep she thought it would be impossible for it to get out again. As she stood there, though, in that cave—which kept switching between the first one, a shelter from the snow, back to the modified one—she could hear it rumbling beneath her. There was a way out, a way up.

The lift. That same lift which had taken her down, would bring him up again. Even now she could hear it, those doors opening.

She understood it was a dream, that all this was . . . was in her mind. But that was where they'd grappled before and she'd won. Or thought she had—

You call this world, the one they *created, winning?*

Where they'd done battle. On the estate, at the cabin. In the cave.

The cave with the lift . . . No, no. Not that one. It hadn't had a lift, they hadn't been invented back then. She was just getting confused again. Or someone—some*thing*—was trying to confuse her. Keep her permanently puzzled, on the back foot.

Where was she? Where had she been? Running, hiding? Fighting? She couldn't for the life of her remember.

For the life of . . .

Already dead, just too stubborn to admit it. Too afraid.

Stop. Just stop. Please, make it stop!

Couldn't remember. Could remember nothing right at that moment. No, that wasn't true. She recalled one thing. That they were coming on and on. Coming for her. Coming to get her. All of them.

Or just one of them. Just *Him*. Rising, rising. Coming for her. Coming to kill her.

CHAPTER SIX

S HE WAS DEAD. THEY'D KILLED HER.

No, not them—not all of them anyway. Just him. Just the torturer, Waterhouse. She'd been close to it when she asked to speak to Tommy, they'd all been able to see it. Not that any of them would have shed a tear (not really) for that monstrosity, so badly damaged from Waterhouse's attentions. Not after almost losing Pat back there.

He'd been the one to hold Peel back, Tommy; grabbing his arm when he was about to rush out. Waiting till the last moment, until they were guaranteed to catch one of the things alive. He'd almost gone himself a few times, poised, tensing. Unable to bear watching Pat, terrified and exposed, whether it was an act or not (definitely not at the end). But he'd held off, knowing why she was risking everything. That it was her idea, as crazy as it was, and she wouldn't thank any of them for putting a stop to it when they were so close.

And it was that holding off which had almost got her killed. As the pack approached, slowly to begin with, crawling forward as if sensing that this might be a trick. Then suddenly surging, leaping at their victim more quickly than anything Tommy had seen in his life. He let go of Peel and they leaped themselves, seeing Waterhouse do the same on the other side—all of them drawing their weapons: the man in black with his rifle, Peel with that axe of his (exactly why he'd experienced a twinge of recognition when he held that, a feeling of loss when he handed it over to its rightful owner, he still didn't know) and Tommy with his automatic pistol.

Pat was seconds away from being torn into, from being torn apart. A claw was descending even as they broke cover, as they sprang into action themselves—and a bullet was waiting for the wolf closest to Pat. Tommy hadn't even had to think about it, he'd simply reacted: aimed and fired. Then Peel was in amongst them, whipping that axe left and right—and once more Tommy felt like it should be him brandishing that weapon.

"Waterhouse! *Now!*" he shouted across to the man, who was already aiming. There weren't silver bullets in his gun, but tranqs—and not one, but three of these found their home in a wolf who was breaking off from the others. Even with those in it, still the thing came, and it took another couple to actually fell it. That meant the field was clear now just to tidy up, take down the rest before they were able to 'call out' for assistance. Tommy shot another in the head, while Peel continued to relieve a couple more of their limbs, before separating their heads from their bodies.

Tommy crouched down next to Pat, eyes scanning her to make sure she wasn't wounded, aside from the intentional one Waterhouse had inflicted on her. He said her name, but she didn't reply to him; was just staring out ahead. When he touched her shoulder she jumped, gaping at him with wide eyes. Then she fell into his arms, and that felt like the most natural thing in the world to him; almost as natural as holding that axe. Pat was shaking, her whole body trembling with fright.

"It's okay," he told her, even as she burst into tears once more—saturating his jacket and t-shirt. "It's over. It's all over."

Except it wasn't. It was far from over.

In fact it was just beginning.

First they had to get out of there, in case any of the wolves had got off a distress signal. The whole area might be swarming with them soon, so Tommy helped Pat to her feet. Even as Peel joined them again, she was regaining her composure; couldn't let the man she so clearly looked up to see she how scared she was.

"You all right?" he asked her and she nodded. "That was a close one. *Too* close, if you ask me."

Tommy could feel Pat shaking again. She hadn't needed a reminder of that, of how close to death she'd come. To divert the attention away from it, he told Peel to help Waterhouse. "Let's get that dog back to the car." And then he'd torn some material from his sleeve and tied it around Pat's leg.

"Jesus, it's heavy," Peel complained as he took the wolf's legs, Waterhouse grabbing it under the arms to heft the dead weight. "And it stinks!"

"Of course it does," said Waterhouse. "You've been this close to them before and never smelt them?"

"I never stick around long enough to really appreciate the bouquet, mate!" came the terse reply.

Tommy helped Pat along, retracing their steps and making their way back to the vehicles as quickly as they were able. Now they could all see why Tommy had insisted on the estate car, as Peel and Waterhouse bundled the wolf into the back. "Right, follow me," he said to them, as they got into the car themselves. He swung one leg over his bike and gunned the engine, setting off to the place he had in mind for the next part of the mission.

He'd come across it a while ago, actually. Perfect for something, he just didn't know what at the time. An old warehouse, fairly secluded, that looked like it had seen better days even before the apocalypse. There was lots of space still inside, though; might have made a good hideaway way back when, or secret base of operations.

Today, it was going to be their prison . . . with one inmate.

Peel and Waterhouse carried the wolf from the car to the building, dumping it inside: in the middle of the empty space that had probably been used for storage. Before they started properly, Tommy got Waterhouse to stitch up the wound he'd given Pat—which had more or less stopped bleeding anyway—and gave her fluids. Then Waterhouse dosed her with the same musk they were all wearing to mask their scent.

"Can't be too careful," the man said. "That way there'll be no interruptions from unwanted guests. Which reminds me . . ." He took a small electrical device out of his pocket, flicking the switch on the side; a red light lit up on the top.

"What's that?" asked Peel.

"A little something I came up with myself. This will stop the creature from communicating with any of its kind who might be around outside this room."

"How's that?"

Waterhouse sighed. "There's a long, technical explanation involving high-pitched frequency waves, but all you need to know, Mr Peel, is that it's been tested out and it works."

"W-Will it hurt the . . . Will it hurt it?" This was Pat.

"It won't do it much good, that's for sure," Peel chipped in.

Waterhouse waved a hand. "It won't interfere with what we want to do, but yes. It'll suffer quite a severe headache." He smiled that chilling grin again. "But that'll be nothing compared with what's to come."

"Good," said Pat flatly, and folded her arms with a nod.

Next Waterhouse brought in the rest of the 'tools of this trade' as he called them, housed inside a case. But he also fetched three of sets of silver chains, the ends of which had manacles attached; the other ends had hinges which he bolted to the ground with what looked like an old battery-powered drill. "It has multiple purposes," he told them, removing the bolt attachment. Then he fixed the still unconscious mutt to the spot with the manacles: one for each wrist and a larger one around the neck.

"How much longer do you figure it'll be out?" asked Tommy.

Waterhouse looked at his watch, lips moving while he made a few calculations. "Shouldn't be too long now. It's a strong one, this—took more than the usual amount to put it under in the first place. Drugs'll work their way out of its system pretty quickly."

"But we're safe, right?" asked Peel, walking around it.

"Don't worry, with all that silver it'll be as weak as a kitten . . . or perhaps I should say a puppy?" He grunted a laugh. "Won't even be able to 'shift. And it won't have much range of movement, which will make my job that much easier."

"You keep calling it a job," said Peel. "Mine was to track and help catch this thing, but what then? What are you going to do?"

"Waterhouse is going to find out what the hell's going on with those freaks," Tommy replied. "Then we can figure out if we'll be able to stop it."

And that was that for a while. They waited once more, not for the monsters to arrive, but for one of their kind to wake up. When it did finally stir, it started to growl. When it opened its red eyes and saw the humans surrounding it, the beast tried to rise—intending to kill every single one of them. The chains, the manacles, all prevented that from happening, as well as significantly weakening the creature. Nevertheless, they all took a few steps back.

Everyone except Waterhouse, that was. He stood there smirking, then said: "Showtime!"

He warned them before he began that his sessions wouldn't be pleasant, but he was actually selling himself short. They were *horrific*, starting off slow: shooting what looked like tiny silver darts into the hound, sapping its strength even more; pulling out each claw in turn with pliers as it howled in pain. Then moving on to the proper slicing and dicing, utilising all those tools of his particular trade, small and large: the drill came into play again with other attachments, as did various spikes, knives and scalpels. At one point Waterhouse was using what looked like a silver machete, hacking into the beast from behind, before squirting some kind of brown liquid on the wounds; possibly vinegar. The savage grin remained fixed to his face throughout all this, as he asked question after question: demanding to know what the wolves were up to; then coaxing it to talk by promising he would stop the torture if it did. He'd been right when he said to Peel that he didn't know what an interrogation was. But this was so much more than that. Brutality beyond anything they'd ever seen. At least the mutts killed you quickly. And this one would glace up periodically, those red eyes looking so sad—if that were at all possible. Pleading with the rest of them to stop this madman.

Peel was the first to leave the room, but Pat soon followed. Even Tommy had to admit that, as much as he hated them, he was starting to feel sorry for this animal. When he couldn't take any more, either, he went outside as well.

Only Pat was around, sitting crossed-legged on the bonnet of the estate car and sipping a drink. He walked over to her. "Where's Peel gone?"

"Went to take a leak," she informed Tommy, putting down her cup.

"I see."

She nodded past him, back towards the warehouse. "How do you know it'll talk? *Can* they even talk in that form?"

"They can, if they want to. And it will. I've never known Waterhouse to fail yet."

"With humans," Pat reminded him. "Not with . . ." She shook her head.

There was silence for a moment or two, then Tommy broke it with: "Look, what you did back there. It's—"

"It was nothing," she told him.

"Wasn't nothing. It was definitely *something*."

"It needed doing. You . . . we needed information." She looked down again, possibly thinking about what was still going on inside that building? No, it was something else.

So that was it, she'd done it for him. Almost got herself *killed* for him. Tommy didn't know how he felt about that right now. He liked Pat, liked her *a lot*. Didn't really understand her, but wasn't that part of her charm? They'd been mates for a while now, but something had changed lately. There was something else in her eyes when she looked at him, as if she wanted to tell him something. Or ask him something. And when she'd been in grave danger back there . . .

"Peel . . . he says that you know," she came out with suddenly, breaking into his thoughts.

"Know what?" asked Tommy.

"About me. That I'm not . . . I mean, that I'm . . ."

Tommy couldn't help it, he let out a small laugh and she looked up at him then, a faint scowl on her face. He apologised. "I didn't . . . You're talking about the girl thing, right?"

"Don't call me that," she said.

"What, a girl? That's what you are though, isn't it?" He was confused now. "I know you prefer to . . . You identify as . . . and that's your choice, but—"

"I'm . . . I'm not a *little* girl, Tommy."

Now he understood. "Right, got it! I'm with you. Not a gender thing. God, I just meant you were . . . You're like what now, sixteen, seventeen?"

"Almost eighteen," she said defiantly, then her shoulders slumped.

"Right, of course."

"I'm not that much younger than you."

"Yeah. I know." And in this world, you grew up fast. You had to. "That wasn't what . . . Look, if you're asking me how long I've known you were . . . Well, it was just obvious to me."

"It *was*?" She seemed surprised by this.

"Yeah." Tommy thought about adding, 'you're not that good an actor' but he knew a lot of blokes—people who barely even registered Pat was around—took her for the opposite sex. Didn't care either way. Instead, to make her feel a bit better, he said: "You're . . . well, you're pretty, Pat."

It took a moment or so, as if she was deciding whether this was a good thing or not, but then she beamed—and there was no mistaking now what she was. That smile lit up their dark and depressing surroundings. "All those chats, why didn't you ever mention anything?"

"It's not something you just casually bring up. How'd you start that conversation: so, you want to be a guy?"

"I didn't . . . I never wanted to be . . . That wasn't . . ." Pat gave up trying to explain and shook her head. It was obviously complicated.

"I just figured you didn't want to talk about it." Tommy leaned on the car, facing her. "Why didn't *you* say anything?" It was a fair enough question.

"I-I was scared to. I didn't want to lose you as a friend."

It was his turn to smile now. "That wouldn't have happened, Pat. You're one of the few people I can actually talk to, confide in."

"So . . ." She looked down at her fingers, picking at the skin from the edge of one. "Is that why you never . . . y'know?"

What was she asking him, why he never made a move? Apart from her wanting to be the opposite sex, or so he thought (which was absolutely fine with him by the way, he had no time whatsoever for small-minded bigots; it was just that he happened to be straight), there had been the age thing. In spite of what she thought, she *had* only been a kid when they first met. Not that he'd been grown up or anything, about the age she was now and so desperate to prove himself that was all he could think about. But on top of everything, there was the threat of being killed hanging over their heads every single day. Friendship was one thing, this would have been something else entirely . . . Lack of focus like that might have got them both killed all the quicker. He rubbed the back of his neck, not sure how to respond to her question. Or how to answer it in a way that wouldn't get him into more trouble.

Before he could say anything, Pat was talking again. "Tommy, listen. If I don't say this now I never will. I—"

"*Tommy!*" Waterhouse's voice cut through the conversation. He was at the door of the warehouse, beckoning him over.

Pat's shoulders slumped again and she sighed. Tommy couldn't decide whether he was relieved at the interruption or sad. "I'd better . . ." he said.

"You go," she told him. "It's all right."

"I'm sorry," he said and meant it. Then he rushed back over to the torturer, to see what was so urgent.

"I got a response. She says she'll only talk to the person in charge," Waterhouse informed him. "That would be you. And she wants to speak alone."

"She?"

"It's a bitch," Waterhouse confirmed.

"Right, okay," said Tommy. "Thanks."

He stepped past Waterhouse, glancing back briefly at Pat as he did so. She was watching him, sadness in her own eyes. Then she looked away, breaking the connection—allowing him to focus as he so badly needed to now. Tommy sighed, and walked through the door.

The creature was even more raddled and broken than the last time he'd seen it, breath coming in short gasps, eyes more doleful than Pat's had been outside. It was also slumped, again a little like Pat was, but this time because it couldn't hold itself fully upright. Its fur was wet in places, matted with dried blood but also from that liquid Waterhouse kept spraying on it. Tommy's stride slowed down, that same fear he felt when he visited his mother returning.

This is what you wanted, he reminded himself. *You needed to know what was going on, and this was the only way.*

"Y-You wanted to speak to me," he said when he was finally near enough, voice cracking. Hardly the voice of a leader, a person in control.

The creature tipped its head, a gesture Tommy took as acknowledgment.

"So, I'm here," he told it, tone strengthening. He was in charge, not this thing.

Its first words to him, when it opened its mouth, were whispered, raspy. Every syllable was an effort, Tommy could see that. "Funny . . ." it—she—managed, "I . . . I thought you'd . . . you'd be taller."

"Excuse me?"

The wolf let out what could only be described as part-growl, part-laugh. "The . . . the great . . . great Tommy Daniels."

She knew who he was. How did she know who he was? Tommy cast his mind back over their time here; had anyone mentioned his name? Waterhouse had called to him outside, but well out of ear-shot—although this thing's hearing would be incredible. Had maybe even heard the conversation outside between him and Pat? So, she might have got he was Tommy, but not *who* he was. Had word spread throughout their ranks as well as his own? He decided to let that pass for a moment, there were more important things at stake.

"Tell me what's going on out there? What—"

"Secrets." She hissed this like a snake would. "Not so . . . secret secrets. Secrets and lies, Tommy."

Bloody Hell, it was like having a conversation with his mother.

The wolf cocked its head. "I-I knew her, you know."

"Knew who?"

"You . . . your mother." The creature began to cough, long and hard—spitting out a mixture of sputum and redness at the end, as a full stop. Then she fixed Tommy with a glare. "I . . . I wasn't always like this."

"You . . . What the fuck are you talking about?" That had thrown him again, the confidence vanishing in an instance.

"S-Steph." Once again, the sound was almost reptilian rather than mammal. The effect was surreal and quite disturbing. "I . . . At least I think that was my name . . . or her name . . . It gets muddled sometimes when you share . . . feelings . . . thoughts, memories."

They all did that, could pass those on. Didn't mean this was the Steph his mother had once talked about so fondly, *her* best friend.

"She . . . she did this to me. To her."

Tommy frowned.

"You . . . you really don't know, do you?"

"Know what? You're not making any sense."

"She . . . she never told you . . . told you the story? Not even as a bed . . . bedtime tale. A fable . . ." The wolf began coughing once more, wheezing as she struggled on with the conversation. "Bad Rachael. Rachael Elizabeth . . . Daniels."

His mother's middle name, how could . . . But then he remembered the channelling thing. Collective memories. Steph—the real Steph—would have known. Waterhouse might have cut off this beast's ability to call for help, to communicate with her own kind, but answers like that were already in its blood. Shared pasts, shared histories. Still, he protested. "You don't know a thing about me or my family."

That laugh again. "You . . . you tell yourself that. While you're at it, you ask her. Ask her about . . . the night they . . . they met. Denim . . . denim on denim . . . I . . . Steph was there."

His dad. Was she talking about his dad? That was the same phrase his mother had used the last time he'd seen her. "My father?"

"One . . . one of them."

She was trying to get to him, and it was working. Trying to mess with him, get inside his head. Literally, it would seem—because her face was screwed up in concentration now, summoning up the strength to do something. And he saw flashes in his mind; blurry images of a place with lots of people inside. It was noisy, they were drinking. Tommy remembered bars from when he was younger, but they'd been family pubs, the only places his mother could take him. This was different, they were all adults here. Someone was staring across the room, staring with oh-so blue eyes. Eyes like his. Wearing . . . a denim jacket, jeans. Nursing a pint, watching. There was noise now, more noise. Someone was fighting, a brawl breaking out. Tommy turned to see someone who looked like his mother, but younger. Another woman with her and—

The wolf slumped again, breathing even more heavily than before. Was she . . . had she been projecting that into his mind? Was that a trick they didn't know about, to pass information on to humans?

Another laugh. "You . . . you really don't have the fir . . . first clue, do you?" she gasped.

"So, tell me," he urged her—no, practically begged her.

"He's buried so . . . so deep. But he'll . . . he'll be free again soon. T-Those mirrors won't help. He's coming back Tommy . . . Then you'll know all about family."

He moved even closer, almost reached out and shook the animal. "Tell me!"

"Operation Wolfshead," the creature said, loudly and clearly.

Tommy took a step back again. "Where did you hear that name?"

"Not . . . not so . . . secret secrets," she repeated.

Had she plucked it out of his head when she'd been planting those images inside? Didn't matter, he told himself, nobody knew the whole plan. Only a handful of people even knew what it was called. Tommy certainly didn't have the vaguest idea about the rest, the details. The where, when and how.

"We . . . we know," The wolf assured him, again as if reading his thoughts. "And . . . and we're ready . . . We'll be waiting . . ."

"No," said Tommy. "No!"

The wolf laughed one final laugh, then coughed again—deep, throaty coughs, worse than ever. With one final effort, it barked then slump over. Unconscious or dead, Tommy had no idea. He ran back to the door, calling out for Waterhouse, who was there in seconds. Pat followed not long after that and they all stood looking at the thing.

"It's not breathing," she said, stating the obvious.

She. She was dead, thought Tommy. They'd killed her. The thing who'd identified as Steph, who may or may not have been his mother's old friend from before he was born.

Waterhouse walked towards the mass of fur. "At least tell me you got what we needed to know, after all that."

"I . . . I got some of it," said Tommy.

The torturer looked back at him and nodded. "That's something, I suppose."

What happened next, happened fast. While his attention was on Tommy, behind Waterhouse the monster was stirring. Changing. Getting smaller. Though it shouldn't have been able to, weakened as it was by the silver and the amount of wounds inflicted—though as Tommy realised after the fact, it could always have made things look much worse than they really were—the wolf was morphing. Shapeshifting. In the blink of an eye, she wasn't even a wolf at all, she was human. She was a naked human woman; the woman Tommy had seen in that pub. In his mother's old photos. The woman called Steph. It still didn't mean it was her, but that didn't matter. What mattered was the manacles at her wrists fell off, tightened as they had been on the much larger creature. Seconds later, she'd undone the clasp on her neck, freeing herself.

Seconds after that, she'd turned back into the wolf—shaking herself, shaking off all the silver which was still attached to her, like a dog shaking off water after a dip in the ocean. Still probably not up to full strength ("It's a strong one, this . . ."), the wolf was strong enough to reach out and grab Waterhouse before he could even react.

The torments of the last few hours were repaid in full then, as the beast pulled both his arms out of their sockets without breaking a sweat. Geysers of blood fountained from the holes at both his shoulders, a look of complete shock and surprise on the torturer's face.

Then the wolf pulled his body in two different directions, torso flying off to the left, legs—limp and useless—off to the right. As she bounded forwards, the wolf brought up a hand to show the claws were growing out of each finger; re-growing in fact, being replaced. Ready to do untold damage.

Tommy's pistol was up and out, but his shot went wide as the creature barged into him, sending him flying. When he landed, he looked up in time to see the wolf stalking Pat. The other hand . . . paw now . . . had its claws back again as well, and it was reaching out, about to cleave her to bits—when it stopped dead in its tracks.

Completely dead, actually, an axe having landed at the base of its neck. Another chop, and the female wolf's head was cleaved off instead. It rolled across the floor to land not far away from where Tommy lay. As the rest of its body toppled, he saw Peel standing there, pulling the axe—which was still dripping with gore—back again, completing the motion.

Pat ran to the man and he let one of the hands he'd been holding the axe with fall, drawing her to his side, taking her under his wing. They were both looking over at Tommy, but he was looking at the object in front of him. Dead, she was dead. They'd . . . Peel had killed her, just not in time.

And all he could think to himself was: wolfshead.

Operation Wolfshead.

CHAPTER SEVEN

THE OPERATION WAS UNDERWAY.

His operation: Wolfshead. They were finally—yet suddenly—putting it into effect, and his name would go down in history because of it. Grice, they'd say, hero of the hour. The end of this oppression, the end of the war, more or less . . . all down to him. He'd succeed where all the governments and all the military endeavours had failed in the past. A concerted effort, a concentrated attack on the very heart of their territory. Co-ordinated, but only he knew the big picture. It was why they couldn't possibly see it coming, because he'd kept that information to himself.

Smaller base commanders knew a little, but not much. And the call had gone out so swiftly that there would be no time for them to mount any kind of defence against his forces. Grice had known for some time where they were, thanks to a messenger who'd stumbled across their main base and lived to tell the tale. Hadn't lived for very long, though, afterwards; such was the necessity to keep that information a secret. By the end, only Grice had known that particular location.

"Teeming with the fuckers," had been that man's description of the place. All it would take would be one strike, with as many numbers as they could muster. Bring together as many fighters as they could—most of them in fact—and end this once and for all.

Messengers had been sent out with the rendezvous co-ordinates, and from there the plan would be outlined before moving on to the actual target. Nothing left to chance, no possibility of leaks at all. Everyone knew the word would be coming at some point about something big, but didn't know the ins and outs. But now, as the convoy headed towards its destination—Grice travelling in an APC towards the back (not wanting to miss the final victory, but at the same time not prepared to be on the front lines of it)—was he starting to have his doubts?

They were tiny niggles, if so, and more than likely down to that pain in the arse Tommy Daniels. Grice was well aware that it had been an unpopular decision to come out here at all without that man. And while he had to agree the boy could certainly fight, he was also extremely good at stirring up trouble. That was the last thing they needed any more of today. Besides, how could he have brought the lad along after what he'd done; just wasn't right. It was insubordination, pure and simple.

Not only had he gone AWOL, gone off half-cocked with that bloody tracker, some wild notion of capturing one of those creatures and pumping it for information in their heads—were they insane?—and in the process had got one of their best operatives killed, but there was also what had happened afterwards to consider.

When they'd returned, Daniels had been brought to his office to explain himself.

"I kept trying to tell you, sir: something's going on out there. Something's not right. I needed to find out what."

Grice had risen and slammed his fist on his desk. "It wasn't your place, soldier! Those aren't decisions for you to make on your own." And wasn't that also the problem with Daniels. Not only did he bend the rules, refuse to follow orders on occasion, he did it because he thought he knew better. Because he thought he was in charge—and might be one day, unless Grice stamped on it now. Couldn't have that drip's name going down in history rather than his.

"The attacks on the smaller bases were just the start of it, sir."

"The start of what?"

"Our extermination," Daniels had replied.

Grice's left eye had narrowed as it had a tendency to do whenever he was angry or stressed. "You persuaded a good man to go with you, and you got him killed for no reason."

"Not for no reason," the boy had argued. "We found out that they know about our plans."

"Impossible!"

"No, not impossible. That thing back there mentioned Wolfshead, sir."

And that had given the general pause for thought, he had to admit. But the codename could have been picked up anywhere—several people knew the grand plan's title, including Daniels. Not one of them knew the plan itself; what it entailed. "They don't know a thing," Grice responded. "We've been putting out misinformation, truth hidden amongst the lies. Even in cases where they've managed to intercept messages—or even obtain the codes to translate them—they wouldn't be able to sort the wheat from the chaff."

Daniels shook his head. "I'm telling you, somehow they know what you have in mind."

"Only one person knows that, and you're looking at him," Grice had shouted back, tapping his head. "And I can assure you, I'm not one of those fuzzy bastards."

"Look, I don't know *how* they know, but I believe it. You have to trust me on this, sir."

Grice had rounded the desk and stepped up to Daniels at that point. "This is nonsense, and if you persist with your current course I'll have no option but to confine you to your quarters."

Daniels had mumbled something then and that had been the last straw for Grice. He'd grabbed the lad by the collar and pulled him forwards, only for Daniels to bring up his own arms and lever himself free. The next thing Grice knew, he was being thrown backwards onto his desk, with Daniels about to punch him. "Guards! Guards!" he shouted and seconds later there were armed men inside the room, pulling Daniels off Grice.

"I'm trying to stop something terrible from happening!" shouted the boy. "At least hold off until we know more, Grice! Why won't you listen to me?"

"Because you're full of shit!" Grice replied, straightening himself and his clothes up. "Lock him in his room until he cools off!"

That's where he'd remained for the time being, under guard—and that's where he'd been when they set out from 1A, something like 80% of their compliment in tow. Had that confrontation been the catalyst for sending out the orders, for getting on with this so quickly? Maybe it had contributed to the speed of it, before anyone could complain or demand Tommy be freed to go with them (would he even have obeyed that command if it had come from Grice?).

Didn't matter, wheels were in motion and there was nothing Daniels or anyone else could do to stop it. This would be an extermination all right, but it would be them doing the exterminating. Getting rid of humanity's greatest enemy forever.

Grice glanced around at the armed men in the back of the APC with him, then looked out of the window. They were getting closer, had encountered no resistance so far—which just reinforced the notion that those fucks didn't have a clue what was about to happen.

They passed by what had once been a central park in the city; Grice had known it well, used to walk his dogs in there every Sunday. Stopping every time to pay his respects to the . . . Yes, it was still there (mostly), the statue of a soldier standing, rifle by his side; a plaque of names at his feet. A monument to those killed in previous wars, remembered for their valiant sacrifice. Those they lost today—and there would always be losses, no matter how small he was expecting them to be—would be remembered with a similar statue once they'd won. Once things had started to get back to normal. Grice didn't want his name on one of those. Wanted, instead, to be remembered very differently.

He hadn't asked for this command, it had come to him when his predecessor had shown weakness and ended his own life. Grice had stepped up, led them and kept them alive so far. Would lead them to this victory and be remembered as the person who brought them out of the wilderness into the light.

Tommy Daniels wasn't the second coming, wasn't even fit to lick Grice's boots. In the end, history was written by the victors—and he would make sure they got it right.

Make sure he himself was honoured properly as society began to rebuild itself once more. He allowed himself a smile at that. This would be the day everything turned around, a tipping point.

And his name would go down in history because of it.

✌

It just wasn't right, any of it.

As Ridgeway made his way inside, beyond the perimeter of their target—heading up a squadron of soldiers, which was happening on all fronts for maximum effect—he was beginning to get an uneasy feeling.

No, that wasn't true. He'd had an uneasy feeling since they'd set off from 1A a couple of hours ago, then met up with other forces to mount this full scale attack on their enemy. The plan had only been explained in broadstrokes, the location still kept a secret from everyone apart from their scouts—who were tasked with finding a quiet route to this place.

But his main doubts were probably to do with the fact that Tommy wasn't with them. He'd become a sort of good luck charm, not to mention someone who always pulled their fat out of the fire if things got a little messy. More than a little, sometimes. Rumour was he'd gone off on some unauthorised mission or something, had even got the interrogator Waterhouse killed—and Ridgeway had been pretty bent out of shape about that. Not because he'd particularly liked Waterhouse (he couldn't think of many people who did), but because Tommy hadn't asked him to be involved.

Probably because he didn't want him getting into trouble, that's what Ridgeway told himself when he heard the news anyway. Because Tommy had certainly got himself in the shit this time. Command had mostly looked the other way in the past when he did something he shouldn't, but this one had been different. And Ridgeway had also heard that Tommy beat up Grice or whatever? Christ . . . There was no way that prissy old fart would let that go. He wasn't quite sure why they kept on following him anyway, other than he'd been the next in the chain of command. As young as he was, Tommy seemed the obvious choice as leader—but that wasn't going to happen, at least for now. And definitely not if this all worked out the way Grice wanted it to.

But he wasn't going in with them, was safe back there in an APC somewhere while the rest of their vehicles encircled this place. While Ridgeway and his company continued to make their way into the middle of the lion's den, quite literally given where they'd found themselves. This place had once been the city zoo, back before the world had lost its way. Appropriated by the wolves now, above and below ground; those few they'd spotted on the surface, though, their snipers had already taken out.

Fake cave entrances and bars that used to belong to cages, enclosures, rubbed shoulders with empty tanks that had once contained water and all manner of aquatic life. If this all went to plan, when they reached the wolves it would be like shooting fish in a tank as well. Or sitting ducks, just waiting for them to let loose with silver bullets and explosives. They'd have no idea what hit them!

So why were Ridgeway's palms sweating so much, why was his forehead so damp? Because they were going down tunnels to get to the centre of the park, the whole thing like spider's web . . . no, more like a spider's body: each team going along a leg to reach the abdomen. He thought back now to that fantasy movie he used to like, used to watch with his kids; where the little fellas were facing that giant spider armed with only a bright light and a tiny sword. Why did it feel like they were doing the same thing, even though they had the advantage on this occasion?

Why did it feel more like they were the flies about to get stuck in the spider's lair?

Those little blokes had won out, though, hadn't they? In the movie . . . Man, he missed moves; missed things like this being fantasy instead of real life. Anyway, they'd won in the end, so why shouldn't their side

now? Because real life wasn't a movie, and terrible things happened—
had already happened. Ridgeway shook the thoughts of his children
away, of what had happened to them. But held on to the anger, the need
for revenge that had fuelled his actions ever since that day.

*Not the blood though, don't think about that. Shut out those walls
covered in redness, the screams—*

Time to end this, time for their *kind* to end. Time . . . He looked
at his watch again, the third check in as many minutes; knew that all
the teams would be emerging from the tunnels at the same moment.
A co-ordinated attack on the wolves that were down here; a reversal of
what they'd done to so many of their own bases recently.

Then he saw it, a shadow up ahead of them. A shape on the wall
. . . A wolf in the tunnel, turning and scampering back to go and warn
the others in the centre. Ridgeway motioned for the rest of his squad
to advance, rifle up and ready. The lone wolf racing to let its comrades
know of the attack would be the first to buy it.

He pulled up short when he reached the exit, which opened onto a
circular walkway, ringing the space down below. The wolf had jumped
from the walkway to land beneath them, as were other wolves at the
rest of the exits all around. One for each tunnel, one for each of their
squads sent down here to get rid of the vermin.

But, as Ridgeway followed its trajectory, he saw that these wolves
were alone. A handful of them down there, while more and more of
his own side's troops were pouring in, jostling each other for position
on the walkways—backed up into the tunnels. More of his kind than
theirs, so many more.

And down there, under this zoo, in the very heart of it—where there
should have been dozens and dozens of wolves, perhaps hundreds,
just waiting to be killed—was a box. A large, black box with some kind
of monitor on the side. The wolves scattered around it were laughing;

more like hyenas than canines. Ridgeway squinted to see what was on that monitor, then realised they were numbers in crimson. Numbers counting down, a timer activated by one of the wolves who'd jumped into the area below.

That wasn't right either, like the rest of all this. No Tommy, no good luck. The worst luck in fact. They were the flies, the fish—and whatever else creatures there had once been in this place. There was no point even raising the alarm, telling the rest of the men from his squadron and all the others that it was a trap; that it had been all along. No point, with so little time left on that clock.

He raised his rifle, got off one shot at least—killing the wolf that had led them down this tunnel. It gave him a certain amount of satisfaction, picturing the faces of his dead son and daughter, just before the numbers reached zero.

Before everything in that underground space turned white, then yellow.

Then red.

ひ

The explosion rocked the ground beneath them.

They all felt it in the vehicles, rippling like the surface of lake when a stone is cast in it. Grice was up and out of his seat, rushing to a window, could hardly believe his eyes when he saw the explosion ahead. It pushed up and outwards; a volcano erupting.

"What's happening?" he cried out, staring from the windows to the men in that APC with him. His protection, should anything go wrong—though not one of them could protect him from this. His eyes were drawn back to the blast, and he saw various details as if in slow motion. Figures rushing from the zoo, attempting to escape the flames that were chasing them and failing miserably. The vehicles surrounding this place blowing up one after the other, like poppers at a birthday party. The hole that explosion had made in the ground itself, pulling everything into it—not a volcano this time, but a swamp sucking everything under that it hadn't already roasted. "Driver, get us out of here!" Grice was screaming now. "Get us the fuck—"

But the driver was already doing that, putting it into reverse, backing up the APC in an effort to escape both the fire and the darkness, both of which were spreading exponentially it seemed.

Grice was shunted forwards then backwards, sent stumbling along the length of the APC past troopers who had remained seated, secured by their seatbelts. He hit the back doors, hard, and struggled for breath. Then as the vehicle moved forwards, he was propelled toward the front again—like he was a ball in a giant game of ping-pong.

He'd barely had time to recover and get his bearings when the APC rolled, onto its side and then its roof. He fell left and right this time, up and down; that same ball placed inside a giant tumbler in a game of bingo.

Over and over it went, the soldiers who were strapped in smashing their heads back against the sides. A jagged piece of metal tore away and flew at one trooper in front of Grice, completely shredding his face, leaving his tongue to loll out of the side that wasn't ruined.

"Shit! *Shit!*" shouted Grice as he continued to roll with the APC. It felt like they were never going to stop—and then just as suddenly as it had started, the journey came to an abrupt halt.

He wasn't sure which way up they were at first, then a soldier's dangling leg caught him a blow to the cheek and Grice realised they were on their side. Right-hand side, most probably. There were moans coming from the men who were still alive or still conscious. Grice climbed over a body that was completely still, tried to unlock a seat-belt belonging to one trooper who was still moving. It wouldn't budge. Others were releasing themselves; two, maybe three. Grice peered into the driver's section and saw only redness in there. There was heat, then light, and at first he thought it was the fire outside that had worked its way in. Instead, these were electrical fires on the inside—which could be just as dangerous if one of them ignited the fuel he was smelling.

Snatching up a rifle, Grice began scrambling towards the back doors. Doors that the others were trying to lever open. "Put your backs into it!" he ordered, hardly able to keep the panic from his voice. Then he was jamming himself up against them, pushing as hard as he could.

When the bottom door flopped open, they all fell with it. One of the soldiers who'd been sitting diagonally opposite him—a woman Grice remembered was called Weaver—was the first up and on her feet, waving her own rifle left and right.

Seconds later, she was snatched up into the air—and her legs began dangling as well. Seconds after that, a huge pool of red had gathered below her slack body.

"*Mutts!*" shouted another soldier, also scrambling to his feet but firing indiscriminately. He hit a couple, more through luck than judgement, but then he too was being mauled. Grice got to one knee, almost fell sideways, but then he was up and making a break for it. His bid for freedom.

Looking back over his shoulder, he saw the creatures taking his people apart, entering the APC and feasting on those who were dead or knocked out. The screams from inside told him that those unfortunates were no longer unconscious.

It was all that was left of his army, those being mopped up by the animals. As Grice ran, desperate to escape and more than willing to let the others buy him that time to get away, all he could think was that his plan had been foolproof. Not that Daniels had been right, but that somehow all this had been his fault. He'd been the one banging on about how they knew, and he had to ask himself if that bastard wasn't somehow involved; wondered if he'd maybe tipped them off. The fact that Grice had been the only one who knew the plan, his reason for ignoring Tommy, didn't come into it at all.

Couldn't. Because that would mean Grice was somehow to blame for this debacle. That his name would go down in history all right, but not because he'd saved them all, ended the war. But because he was the cause of their doom.

And that, to him, pure and simple, just wasn't right.

CHAPTER EIGHT

THERE'D BEEN NO WAY TO MAKE THINGS RIGHT.

No way to make any of this all right, let alone what had happened. But he'd done his best, on the drive back to 1A with Pat—who looked for all the world now like the traumatised kid she actually was. In the space of the last few days she'd been through so much, probably more than she'd ever encountered even living on the streets on her own. Back then she'd kept her head down, kept away from danger. She'd done the same when delivering those messages to the smaller bases, avoided the enemy at all costs.

Now she'd faced death—looked it in the eyes, literally—not once but three times. Had almost bought it back at 7B, then again when she'd insisted on being the bait for the hunting mission, and finally when the subject of that mission got loose and killed Waterhouse. Was there any wonder she was in a state of shock?

Not admitting it only got you so far. You couldn't hide how you really felt inside, nor hide it forever from those who cared about you.

When she'd rushed to Peel's side after that last attack—when he'd got there just in the nick of time once again—and he'd held her, he'd known then who she truly was.

How truly scared she was.

Tommy had gone on ahead to scout, same as before, and Peel had been left with little choice but to get behind the wheel of the estate to ferry them both home. He'd made her laugh then, unintentionally it had to be said, by kangarooing the vehicle when he tried to pull out. She hadn't been able to help herself, stifling her chuckle behind her hand. If she had belonged to him, if he really had been her father she might have said:

"Da-aaaaa-d!"

But instead, once they got going properly to begin the journey back home (and yes, wasn't he starting to think of that place as home? It was definitely Pat's), she'd lapsed into silence again. Staring out ahead of her, vacant expression on her face.

When he couldn't stand it any longer, Peel said, "It'll be okay, you know. It'll all be okay."

Pat had turned and gaped at him then, as if he'd been talking Chinese. "No. No, it won't. It never will." Said with the certainty of a child who saw things much more clearly than an adult.

So, that's when he'd told her. That's when he'd tried to make things all right again. It was what . . . what parents did, wasn't it? Partly a distraction, partly to give her some kind of hope, he told her a story. A legend really, something he'd come across on his travels, searching for ways to combat this menace. Ways to defeat them for good.

"Now, don't quote me on this, because I'm not sure any of it is Gospel . . ." Peel glanced across and saw his young companion was no less confused by what he was saying now. "It's a myth, something that's been handed down through generations. You understand what I'm saying?"

She nodded, but he still wasn't sure she did.

"It's about The First Wolf."

That got her attention. "The what?"

"Well, if you think about it, there had to be a first one of these things. Something that kicked everything off, right?"

"I-I suppose. Hadn't really thought about it."

"I did, *a lot*. Thought about nothing else but those things after what happened to me. Knew I wouldn't get my life back until something was done about them, and I guess that still stands today." Peel crunched the gears, and she winced. "Sorry. Little rusty. What was I saying? Oh yeah: The First Wolf. Legend goes that way back, I mean you're talking when humans were first around—that long ago—a man got caught in a blizzard. This bloke, he was hunter, a tracker."

"Just like you."

Peel shook his head. "Not really, but we'll come to that. Half-starving, and seeking shelter, he found a cave, so he did what any of us would have done: he set up camp, made a fire, looked around inside for something to eat.

"Problem was, the man wasn't alone in there. He'd actually taken refuge in a wild animal's cave. A wolf."

"The First Wolf?" asked Pat.

Peel nodded. "Who was around long before we were, maybe even around at the dawn of time itself." He looked over again, saw that Pat was gripped by the tale, and for a moment had a flash of her as a little girl, tucked up in bed with the covers pulled up high; him sat beside her, reading from a book, relating some kind of fairy tale. The kind of life he'd always pictured when he was growing up himself, the kind of life that had been denied him by the monsters he'd hunted for so long.

But it was all connected, and he'd get to that eventually. Peel realised Pat was waiting eagerly for the next bit, that he'd drifted off in his own thoughts.

"What happened next?" she asked, not prepared to wait for him to continue of his own accord.

"What do *you* think?" he said with a smirk. It was the kind of playful teasing he would have done if he'd brought her up.

"Knowing that lot, it would have ripped the living shit out of him." And the illusion that she was anyone's little girl was suddenly and spectacularly obliterated, but he couldn't help laughing.

"It tried, that's for damned sure. Probably did a fair amount of damage, but the hunter fought back. He was weakened from the cold and lack of food, but he did have one secret weapon in his back pocket. Though he didn't realise it at the time, the tip of his spear was made from something that could do the beast quite a lot of damage itself."

"Silver!" Pat shouted, her excitement mounting.

"Bingo. Give that woman a cigar!" Another puzzled frown from Pat. "It means you're right," he informed her and was rewarded with the merest flicker of a smile. "The story goes that when it pounced on him the final time, he punctured its heart and its massive body fell on him, trapping the hunter beneath it. So, there he was, stuck underneath that thing."

"Wait a minute, The First Wolf died? He just killed it?" Pat's voice was rising with intensity.

Peel took one hand off the steering wheel and held it up. "That's not the end of the story, though. As trapped as he was, the hunter was still starving. He hadn't been able to find any food in that cave, and here was an animal he could eat. Maybe it would give him strength."

"He *ate* The First Wolf?"

"Yep."

"What, raw?" Pat was pulling a face.

"You're telling me you've never eaten anything raw?"

Pat thought about her answer for a second. "Well, not completely raw . . . No. That's disgusting. And he could have caught all sorts."

Peel laughed again. "He was desperate, I guess. But no, he shouldn't have eaten it, mainly because it did have an effect on him."

"Probably gave him the trots," Pat added helpfully.

"Not exactly. You see, like I said before this hunter wasn't like me at all. Wasn't like anybody you've ever met. He had a sort of . . . ability, I suppose you'd call it. Like the old superheroes from comics and . . ." He could see that, yet again, she had no idea what he was going on about. "How to put it, he could mimic other people—though he didn't know it until he'd eaten the wolf. Until he began to take on that thing's traits. Absorb its strength, its power."

"*Become* The First Wolf, you mean?"

"In a way, though by all accounts he retained control of it . . . more or less. Locked in a constant battle."

Pat shifted about in the seat uncomfortably. "What happened to him after that?"

"Some say that other legends were based on him. Gods like Anubis from Egypt, Zeus from ancient Greece who could shapeshift at will. King Nebuchadnezzar of the Old Testament . . . The Bible?" Pat had no knowledge of any of these things, hadn't been taught them by her parents, hadn't been to school where she might have learned about them. "Okay, how about this one. Quite a famous fable about a girl who wore a red hood, who visited her grandmother one day only to find the woman had been eaten and a wolf dressed like her had taken her place." That one rang a bell, he could see the recognition in Pat's eyes.

"But . . . but I don't understand, what's all this got to do with defeating *them*?"

"Because," answered Peel, "all these others came from The First Wolf. Shadows of the original, pale imitations. Reflections. Accidents who got away, that kind of thing. I'm not sure what suddenly ramped it up all those years ago, maybe The First Wolf lost control or had to go into hiding? Went underground? Or into hibernation . . . But the virus spread then like wildfire, which is how we got where we are today."

"I still don't—"

"Kill The First Wolf, Pat, and you kill them all," Peel told her matter-of-factly. Like it was the easiest thing in the world to do, like he hadn't been hunting that original wolf all this time, before and after the apocalypse. "Or the virus dies at any rate, perhaps even returns those who've turned to their ordinary selves. There are even some who say that everything will return to normal once that First Wolf is gone. Reset."

Pat's mouth was hanging open when he looked over. She quickly realised and snapped it shut again. "But where . . . How do we find. . .?"

"Now you see, that's the tricky part. I have absolutely no idea. Wish I did. But," he said with a wink, "at least there's a chance. It's something, Pat. It's a slim hope, but it's hope."

She nodded slowly, went back to looking at the road ahead of them, staring out into the distance. And he thought he'd lost her again, the tale not enough to shake her out of this. Then suddenly she said, "I did something about it."

Peel wasn't quite sure what she was referring to, finding The First Wolf? But she was talking past tense and she hadn't even known about the legend before he told her. Then he followed her gaze, up ahead, watching Tommy on the bike—as he weaved about in front—and understood.

"That is, I tried to. I was trying to when . . . all that back there."

"Okay," said Peel, not quite sure what to say.

"I think . . . I think he might feel the same way about me."

"Okay," repeated Peel.

"Maybe when we get back, we can—"

"Okay," he said a third time. "Now, hold on a second. I know I said do something about it, but don't you think all that's just a bit quick?"

"Have a proper chat, I was going to say. Why, what did. . .?" Pat's mouth was open again. "I'm not . . . I hadn't even . . . And Tommy's not . . ." She lapsed into silence again.

Not for the first time, he'd put his foot in his mouth. Reacted again like a parent whose kid was trying to confide in them about her love life, and it had been a knee-jerk reaction at that. "I didn't mean to—"

"You were the one who said go for it!" argued Pat, folding her arms and pushing back into what there was of the seat.

"I didn't . . . I don't think I said it quite that way. I just meant . . . Look, I just don't want you to get hurt."

"You're kidding. Did you just miss all that back there?" Now she was thumbing over her shoulder in the direction they'd just come. "Hurt? I was almost killed. Twice."

He thought about pointing out that he'd been the one stopping that from happening, twice, but thought better of it. "You know exactly what I mean. There are other ways to get hurt, swee . . . Pat. Just be careful, that's all."

"Yeah, I *do* know what I'm doing, but thanks for the advice . . . *Dad.*" Her voice had been dripping with sarcasm when she said it, but she had called him it. Mind you, he'd almost said it again, almost called her by the name he would have called his own daughter if he'd had one. He shook his head and this time the silence lasted till they dumped the vehicles, till they were back at 1A and getting checked over in the lift again, before being relieved of their weapons.

And even though it was absolutely none of his bloody business, he'd been ready to say something in case Pat headed off with Tommy somewhere. Figured she might be willing to do something stupid now just to spite him. Just to prove she did know what she was doing, when she clearly didn't; was not thinking straight. But in the end it hadn't come to that, because Tommy had been whisked off to Grice's office as soon as they returned, no doubt for a telling off.

Pat had also wandered off, not even saying goodbye—and Peel had stood there rubbing his face. He hadn't asked for this, to be a parent to her, and yet apparently that's what he was trying to do. But to be thrown in at the deep end with a teenager . . .

He spotted a familiar face not far away and called out his name: "Eddie! Oi, Eddie." The soldier stopped and turned, holding a hand up in greeting. Peel had trotted over to him. "You said if I ever wanted anything, just to ask."

Eddie nodded.

"Where can a fella get a belt around here?" he asked him.

&

It turned out the answer to that question was nowhere.

The best Eddie had been able to offer him was apple juice, which he took back to his quarters anyway. Maybe if he willed himself to think it, the stuff might taste vaguely alcoholic—or if he waited long enough it would just turn into cider. Peel had sat back on his bunk, staring at the glass of liquid in his hand for what seemed like eternity.

In fact, he was concentrating so hard on the glass that when the knock came he almost spilt it in his lap. Peel put it down on the bedside table, got up and opened the door. He was surprised to see Dr Kingsley standing there on his threshold, white coat on, hands behind her back.

"Hey there," she said.

"H-Hey yourself."

"I . . . well, you skipped out on your check-up after you got back," she told him.

"Another one?"

"Just a check-up, not the full works."

Peel sighed, stepped back. "You'd better come in, then."

She followed, closing the door with one hand. He still couldn't see what she had in the other; he assumed her bag of tricks. As long as it wasn't Waterhouse's.

"You weren't injured then on your little jaunt?" she said, which again reminded him of the interrogator and his death.

"No, just my pride." He gave a laugh but there was no humour to it. "Ended up better than some."

"Oh yes, I heard . . ." Kingsley walked further in. "What on Earth were you doing out there, Peel?"

"Seemed like a good idea at the time," he replied.

"You could have been . . ." The doctor shook her head, her auburn ponytail flicking from side to side. "And when I couldn't find you on the base, I thought you'd gone for good."

"You . . . you were looking for me?"

"Only to . . ." She shook her head again, seeing no point in lying. "I didn't want you to leave so soon. Is that wrong?"

Peel's turn to shake his head. "No. I-I thought about finding you before I left, but . . ."

"But that would have been a bit weird, right? We hardly know each other."

"Yeah," said Peel, looking down, then up again.

For a second or two, neither of them said anything, then Kingsley nodded towards the glass of liquid on the table. "How's the juice?"

Peel screwed up his face.

"It's good for you."

"Hmm."

"But maybe you'd prefer something a little bit stronger?" She brought out what she'd been hiding, a clear bottle of deep brown liquid. "Heard you were looking for . . . how did Trooper Haines put it, a belt?"

Peel grinned. "Haines? You mean Eddie."

"Another reason why I'm here. Do you have a second glass?" she asked, as Peel tipped the apple juice down his sink and washed the receptacle out. He shook his head. "Then I guess we're going to have to share."

Peel offered her a seat, held out the glass for her to pour some of the liquid in. Then he gave it to her. "You first."

She smiled. "A gentleman. You don't get many of those around here."

"Hardly. Actually, I was just making sure it didn't poison me. What is that, rubbing alcohol?" When she frowned he pointed to the bottle. "No label."

"I'll have you know this is fifteen year old malt. No label means that it doesn't go walkabout . . . I've been saving it for a special occasion." She knocked her measure back in one, poured Peel a generous amount.

"Oh, is *that* was this is?"

"Might be, if you play your cards right."

She left that hanging there, and he didn't quite know how to reply. So instead, he sipped the liquid, cocked his head. "Now, that *is* smooth."

"Naturally."

"Cheers." He held up the glass and she clinked it with an imaginary one she held up. "So . . ."

"So?"

"Check-up?" he reminded her, not that he was in any rush.

"Right. Yes. Although in all good conscience would I be able to carry out my duties properly? Now that I'm inebriated and all?"

"You're not . . . *Oh, right,*" he said, drinking more of the liquid, handing the glass back for her to drink the rest.

"If you're willing to take the risk, I guess we could . . ." Kingsley told him. "I mean, as long as you don't tell anyone about it."

"Who would I. . .?"

She laughed, polished off his whisky and poured herself another. "Not very good at this, are you?"

"What, drinking?"

"Flirting."

"Ah, okay . . . To be fair, I haven't done either in a good while."

"All right. So, back to business. If you just want to get your clothes off, and we'll have a look at you."

He paused, frowned. "I thought we were . . . I mean, the flirting. Not doing the whole check-up thing."

Kingsley threw back the next measure. "Who said anything about check-ups? I said I wanted to have a look at you." She laughed.

Peel laughed too, albeit nervously. "I'm pretty sure you've already seen all there is to see."

"Oh, I certainly hope not," replied Kingsley, pouring him another glassful which he accepted graciously. "Come on, big boy. Don't be shy."

Several things went speeding through his head at once, but mainly his own words to Pat, and hers to him:

Don't you think all that's just a bit quick?

Look, I just don't want you to get hurt.

Just be careful, that's all.

I do know what I'm doing . . .

They were both adults, but that didn't mean they knew what they were doing either. Very rarely did. Kingsley had said it herself, they hardly knew each other. Maybe now, and in the days to come, they could rectify that? Maybe he also owed Pat an apology; her private life was exactly that. Private. None of his affair . . . And in this time of uncertainty, maybe they all deserved some happiness.

Because here and now, in front of him, was a strong, intelligent, beautiful woman he couldn't take his eyes off. Who he wanted more than anything in the world.

Someone, thought Peel, who might be able to make everything all right again.

If only for a little while.

CHAPTER NINE

TOMMY WAS FAR FROM HAPPY.

Alone, in his quarters, with nothing to do but bounce off the walls . . . and think. He liked to keep busy, always on the go, always doing something—and in the years since the world broke, that something had been fighting. He'd never liked time to think, to be alone with his own thoughts, let alone someone else's. Because that's what it felt like, that there was someone else in his mind. Ever since he'd talked to the she-bitch back at the warehouse. Ever since he'd been shown a glimpse of his mother's past.

He shook his head, attempting to focus on something else. Pat, maybe? Think about Pat and what she'd been telling him, what they'd started to discuss just before that happened. The feelings that had been stirred up, more intense now than ever before. Not that he could do anything about that, couldn't even tell her while he was locked up inside this room!

Because of Grice. All because of that knobhead Grice, who was in charge. Because he wouldn't listen to Tommy's warnings, thought they were bullet-proof. Thought his plans were watertight. Of course, they might be; could just have been the wolf trying to sow the seed of doubt in Tommy's mind. It's what they did, what they enjoyed doing, playing games with people. But somehow he knew that wasn't the case, felt the truth of the words.

Not so secret secrets . . . Operation Wolfshead.

And he couldn't tell Grice how he knew that, not without compromising himself. Not without getting himself banged up somewhere like this—or worse—for life. Or maybe even executed. But then Tommy wasn't even sure of himself, so perhaps it wasn't such a bad thing for him to be in here for the time being. Maybe he *had* been compromised? The wolf had been in his head, after all—there was no denying that. If they could do that with other humans . . .

Again, he didn't feel like they could. Wasn't a link they shared with just anyone, so why him?

He'd begun to experience more visions while he was riding back here on the bike, of an old woman, an attack on a van . . . Had to push them away, try to bury them deep and focus on the road ahead of him; as it was he'd weaved about a bit too much, almost crashed his bike into a wall at one point. Then, when they'd returned, he'd had other things to distract him—like the confrontation with Grice. The one that had seen him confined to his room with armed guards outside.

With nowhere to go, and nothing else to do but think. His thoughts, someone else's thoughts. Dangerous thoughts. He'd tried his hardest to fight them back again, but still they came. Those visions of the past, his mother's past.

"I knew her, you know . . . Your mother.

"I wasn't always like this . . .

"She . . . she did this to me. To her.

"To Steph . . .

"Where is Steph, anyway? I miss her."

Tommy pounded his temples, trying to drive out the sights he was seeing. A living room, his mum—young again as she had been in the vision of the pub—and her best friend, chatting. His mother recovering from some sort of ordeal.

"Is there something wrong, Stephanie?" she was asking. "Do you *really* want to know what did all of this?"

And in the mirror, the small mirror Steph was holding: a reflection of his mum. Her real face . . .

No, no! One of those things *pretending* to be his mother. Like she'd been saying about his gran, the thing that killed *her*. Taking on Rachael Daniels' appearance to gain entrance to the flat, murdering her in cold blood.

Seeing that now: seeing the redness which had coated that same living room. His gran's lifeless body. Steph hadn't even been there when that happened, though, so how could he be seeing . . .

None of it made any sense.

Suddenly Tommy was flashing back to his father again—when his mother had encountered him the second time. The moment they'd fallen in love, in fact. His mum's memories, these; that bond they'd always shared . . . Yet they'd never shared anything like this. How was it even possible to—

A fight, outside and inside that motel room where his father had met his end. The shattering of glass as his dad was thrown through a window, being flung around in that room like he was nothing, until nearly all the life had left his body. His mother there, confronting the beast—the words it had said to her. An explanation, something Rachael had forgotten.

"He's still there, you know, inside that skin you wear . . . Always will be to some extent. But what there is of him lies dormant, subdued, useless.

"You're just a memory of someone who once was, pretending to be something that shouldn't even exist—simply because you don't know any better . . .

"You're already dead. You're just too stubborn to admit it. Too afraid . . . You could always change, you know—if you wanted to.

"You have it in you. Make this an even match."

Tommy ran to the wall, banged on that instead with his fist. "No!" he screamed. "No, no. *No!*" The link between them, mother and son. But something else, something more. Something he'd always known really deep down. A link they all shared, something in the blood.

Didn't stop there, however. He was treated to a vision of Steph in a white room, a hospital perhaps? Having escaped from her best friend, and got away—though not without paying a price. Feeling those same cravings for blood, for flesh. An infection his mother . . .

It had all begun with her. Everything.

Then his birth, traumatic as it was. She shouldn't have survived it; *he* shouldn't have survived it either. Shouldn't even have been possible, but there he was. A baby in her arms.

"I shouldn't have put you in such . . . You shouldn't even be here, it's not possible. You shouldn't even exist. Neither of us should . . ."

She shouldn't be here because she was dead, because—as she'd once said to her mother—she'd had a dream that she'd been eaten by the beast. Except it hadn't been a dream at all.

"He's still there, you know, inside that skin you wear . . ."

But Tommy shouldn't even be here because—

And you wonder why those wolves stay away from you, back off and don't attack!

Two fathers: one a hunter; one who was also his mother! Jesus Christ . . . Jesus fucking Christ! Not even visible in mirrors because she was in control—

The flash of red eyes the last time he'd seen her.

"*Something's wrong, something's wrong . . . I'm losing my grip, Tommy. He's . . . I can't hold him at bay. Can't hold any of them!*"

"*He's buried so . . . so deep. But he'll . . . he'll be free again soon. T-Those mirrors won't help. He's coming back Tommy . . . Then you'll know all about family.*"

Tommy flung himself against the other wall now, beating on it. Hitting it until his hands started bleeding. But the visions still weren't done. They had one last thing to show him.

Operation Wolfshead.

He saw plans: where, when and how. Written down in spite of what Grice had said, what he'd insisted; tapping his head like that as if it was all up there. At some point they'd been written down, and now he could see them. See everything! A plan escalated by the attacks on the smaller bases, meaning they'd be left with no other choice but to strike at the heart of them now rather than later. A target they couldn't ignore. As Peel had said:

"*Good hunter lures his prey to where they want them, then* bam! *You got anything that they might want? Something they can't resist?*"

Bait.

It had been his fault, all his fault. He'd been the missing link, the sleeper inside who'd passed on the information without knowing it. He was the reason why they were walking into a trap right now! Grice was leading every single one of them to their deaths.

He had to get out of there, find them and warn them that . . . But in his heart of hearts, he already knew it was too late, and who'd believe him anyway? All his fault, all his . . .

Then he remembered the open door. The open door to his mother's mirrored room. He wasn't the only weak link, was he? Could she have crept out and got a look at the plans without anyone noticing? Difficult, but not impossible. Was he clutching at straws?

For fuck's sake, he didn't even know if *any* of this was real or not! That bloody she-bitch could have whammied him somehow. Dosed him with something that would make him think—

In any event, he needed to get out of there. Needed to get to his mum so he could find out for sure what the bloody hell was going on. What the hell had been going on for such a long time, since before he even entered this world.

Tommy began banging not on the walls now, but the door. Screaming and shouting, getting the guards' attention. There were two of them posted outside, good men—Barnes and Willis—comrades in arms who hadn't even wanted to escort him here and put him under 'house' arrest.

"Hey! Hey, can you guys hear me?" Tommy banged again, and this time the door opened.

Barnes was first one through. "What? What's the—" Tommy grabbed the end of his rifle, swinging the man around and into the room, relieving him of the weapon completely. He reeled backwards and fell onto the floor. Willis, who was right behind, was raising his weapon—but Tommy had already turned Barnes' gun around and had it trained on the second man. "Drop it . . . please." The man hesitated, like he was going to try something, but then let his own rifle clatter to the floor. "Inside," motioned Tommy with the end of the gun, stooping to pick up the other one.

"What are you doing, Tommy?" asked Barnes.

"Something I have to do," came the reply. "I'm sorry, I really am." Then he stepped out and locked the door behind him, propping their weapons up against the wall opposite.

Looking left and right, he started to run up the hall—then started to head downwards. He needed to return to the deepest part of this facility, down staircases, down lifts. Until, finally, he was there.

Back in the corridor, only there was barely a hesitation as he strode up it. The door was shut this time, so he banged on it—to be let in now, not out. Or maybe he was giving his mother some warning that he was coming inside, and he wasn't about to take any crap on this occasion.

When nothing happened, he took out the card that would allow him access; swiped it, and let himself inside.

Was he looking for confirmation, for his mum to tell him what he'd been told—what he was seeing—was right? Or did he desperately need her just to say, "Tommy, that's the craziest thing I've ever heard!" and then give him a hug, tell him everything was going to be okay? Either way, he just needed the truth.

As he opened the door, and without either of them having to say a thing, he found it.

And he knew nothing would ever be okay again.

രാ

She kept well back, just as she had done all the way down here.

Just as she had done as she'd camped out watching the door to Tommy's room, knowing full well that neither Willis nor Barnes would let her inside to see him. Waiting . . . for something, she didn't quite know what. Definitely not for Tommy to lock them up after banging and shouting for them to open the door.

Pat had thought about going over to him then; after all he was free now. But there was a look on his face, a determination she'd never really seen before. Not even when they were out there on that mission, and he'd wanted to get to the bottom of the mutts' schemes. Not even when he was arguing about orders he disagreed with, but mostly followed anyway.

So, instead of letting him know she was there, she'd followed him. Followed, just as she had done when he'd been summoned to Grice's office in the first place. Followed, as the two soldiers who'd taken him from that place took him back to his quarters and locked him inside.

Just what in God's name had happened in there? Pat asked herself. Had he attacked Grice or something? It certainly looked that way . . . But that just wasn't Tommy at all!

Then again, neither was all this secrecy. Sneaking around, looking over his shoulder as he headed off somewhere. She'd had no choice but to tag along, keeping well back and making sure he didn't spot her. Taking the lift after he did, then picking up his trail again (she'd learned well from Peel). Until, eventually, he'd arrived at that corridor. At that locked door.

She'd got there just in time to see him stop short and open it. There had been the merest hint of what was inside—mirrors, had that room been full of mirrors?—and then the door was closed again, shutting her out. Not that he knew she was there, of course. Not that he could ever know.

Which was why Pat was retreating again. If Tommy was to come out suddenly, spot her, realise that she'd been spying on him . . . She couldn't even think about that; he'd probably never speak to her again. And that would break her heart.

But at the same time he'd clearly been keeping things from her.

"Pat . . . You're one of the few people I can actually talk to, confide in."

She couldn't help wondering what he was doing. What had been worth breaking out of confinement for. If Grice had been ready to throw the book at him before, then this time he'd chuck an entire shelf . . . no, a library at him!

Even that would be nothing compared to the trouble he was in now, inside that room. Somehow felt that it would affect all of them: her; Peel (and she was still pretty mad with him, even though he was the person she was thinking about seeking out now); everyone on the entire base in fact.

Tommy especially, though. Felt sure his future was being determined in the mirrored room, that it also had something to do with his past.

And she couldn't help wondering whether anything would ever be the same again.

CHAPTER TEN

THEY LAY BACK PANTING. EXHAUSTED, BUT CALM. RELAXED AND content.

The last few hours had been a whirlwind, a storm whipping up out of nowhere that had taken his mind off everything that had happened—not just in the recent past, but since the motel. Since his life fell apart. It had been almost as long since he'd been with *anyone*, so Peel was nervous—as nervous as he'd been when Kingsley started flirting with him in the first place—but she'd taken him in hand (he couldn't help a small chuckle at that), and it hadn't taken too long for them to be comfortable with each other.

And with that comfort had come passion. An eagerness for each other, especially when Kingsley took her own clothes off: her white coat first, then her scrubs and underwear.

"Wow," he'd said, mouth open and gazing at her as she stood there naked in front of him.

"I'll take that as a compliment," she replied with a grin, then pointed down. "That too."

Peel looked as well, reddening. Might have stood there forever had she not made the first move, closing the gap between them, her lips on his, hands roaming his body. Seconds later they were on the cramped bunk, exploring each other—his hand cupping a breast, playing with the nipple till it was hard and she let out a moan. Her fingers stroked his flesh and he bucked at first, then responded eagerly to her touch.

Before he knew it, he was inside her, lying sideways and facing each other—their eyes open, tongues darting in and out of each other's mouths. He hadn't lasted long at all that first time, but they were in no rush Kingsley said. As she guided his hand down, his fingers moving in circular motions, he was already starting to harden again anyway—and before long she was on top of him, hips moving back and forth, teasing him to the point of climax before easing up again. Drawing out the pleasure until he couldn't stand it anymore and rolled her over, thrusting inside again and again as her nails raked his back. This time they both came together, and he collapsed on top of her.

"Wow," he managed again between breaths, and she laughed.

"That's just for starters," Kingsley promised him, and she hadn't been lying. By the time they were finished, there hadn't been a position they hadn't tried, an area of each other's bodies they hadn't sought out with mouths or fingers. Though that last time they simply enjoyed the feel of one another, the sex slow and sensual, leading to an inevitable explosion of pure joy. As they lay back, it was Kingsley's turn to echo him and say: "Wow!"

He looked across at her beside him, so close because there was barely any room on the bunk—though he had a feeling they would have been like that anyway, even if the bed had been enormous. As if neither of them wanted to let go, didn't want this time together to end. For the bubble to burst. "You're so beautiful," he told her then.

"Naw," she said, but smiled. Not the grin from before, but a genuine smile of delight. "I bet you say that to all the ladies you meet in underground bunkers . . . I'm nothing special."

"You are to me." The words were out before he could help himself and he studied her face for a reaction, positive or negative. She was biting her bottom lip, a concerned expression on her face. He shouldn't have gone there, shouldn't have said what was on his mind. Couldn't afford to let feelings like that get the better of him, and neither could she. Stupid, stupid! He quickly changed the subject: "How . . . how *did* you come to be here? What's a nice lady like you doing in an underground bunker like this anyway?"

The smile returned, though it was a little strained. "Came with the territory, when I signed up."

"You . . . you're military?"

"Born and bred. Same as my granddad and dad before me. I was an army brat, me and my mum followed him around all over the place. I just assumed you knew?"

"I . . ." He shook his head. "I don't know why I didn't . . . Maybe it was the doctor thing. I thought perhaps they'd found you, like Pat, out there?"

"I studied medicine, but the army was in my blood before I was even born. There was no way I could fight it. Played havoc with your private life, though, on the road all the time." One thing they had in common, at any rate. She leaned up on an elbow. "Let me guess, it was always a fantasy of yours to make it with a sexy nurse or doctor, but not with a major?"

"A *major?*" Peel gasped.

"What? You have a problem with that?"

Another shake of the head. "Far from it . . . I-I'm impressed." *And would have been even more intimidated if I'd known*, he thought.

Kingsley smiled again, broader than ever. "It's because I can kill you with my little finger, isn't it?" She stuck it up in the air to illustrate her point.

"I preferred what you were doing with it a little while ago."

She gave a chortle. "Don't worry, I won't expect you to salute or anything, or call me Major Kingsley. You're a civilian, if anyone can still be classed as that these days . . . Besides, it's not as if what we were doing was exactly regulation."

"You're telling me," said Peel. "Major Kingsley . . . I mean Dr Kingsley."

"How about we just go with Andrea."

He nodded. "Andrea. I like that."

"And you? I can't keep on calling you Peel forever."

"Most people do," he told her. "Did, I mean. Back when I . . . I had people, that is."

"So, you don't have a first name? You're what, like Bono or Morrissey or something."

"I guess I don't need to ask what kind of music you prefer." That would have all been part of getting to know one another, along with favourite foods, movies . . . Peel wasn't even sure this woman wanted that now. Wasn't even sure if he *should* want it. Before she could think about that too much again, he blurted out: "Noah. There, if you really must know. It's Noah."

She didn't laugh, like all the kids at school had done; didn't make jokes about him having 'no appeal'. She just said: "As in: the animals went in two by two?"

"Mum was pretty religious. Always thought that the world would start over again someday, that God would wipe the slate clean one more time. Guess she figured I'd stand a chance if she called me that."

Kingsley sat up. "Well, she wasn't wrong about the world starting over. Only it wasn't a flood this time."

"Where are you going?" he asked her.

"Duty calls . . . Noah." He groaned, at both the use of his first name and the fact she was leaving him. "I shouldn't really have stayed this long, not with everything that's going on. But I . . . I really enjoyed myself."

"Me too." Peel sat up as well. "Hey, wait, what do you mean with everything that's going on?"

The concerned face came back almost immediately. "I-I'm not sure I should be saying anything really. Not that I know much."

"Come on, Andrea." By contrast, it felt good to say her name out loud. Felt right. "You can tell me."

"All right, but keep it to yourself because that could really get me into hot water . . . There was some sort of push today, Grice was overseeing it himself. Left with most of the base's compliment a good while ago. I'll probably be needed in case there are any casualties."

"Push? You mean they were going up against the wolves?"

"Who else?"

It had to have something to do with what they'd found out, what Tommy had been told by the creature they captured. "I should have gone with them."

"Like I said before, you're still seen as—"

"A civilian, right."

"Count yourself lucky, or you might have ended up getting confined to quarters yourself like your friend." She looked around. "Though I suppose you have been after a fashion, haven't you."

He frowned. "Pat?"

She shook her head, which only left one person; one person who was still alive at any rate. "Then again, if you're going to hang around with Tommy Daniels, sooner or later you're going to end up in hot water."

Kingsley began to get up and he grabbed her by the arm. "What did you just say?"

She looked down at his hand. "You want to let go now?"

He did, apologising, but repeated his question.

"Tommy Daniels. You get what you deserve when you get mixed up with him. Don't believe everything you hear."

"Daniels . . ." Peel was staring hard at her.

"That's right. Why, what did—" But Kingsley didn't get a chance to ask Peel the question, because that's when all the alarms started going off. When the lights went out momentarily, only to replaced seconds later by ones that turned everything crimson.

And that was when they both realised that the time they'd spent together, the calm before the real storm hit, was well and truly over.

CHAPTER ELEVEN

W HAT HAD HAPPENED WAS THIS.

Grice had made it back to 1A, covered in blood. Quite clearly wounded, but insisting, screaming at the electronic voice that was
questioning him at the entrance that they weren't the result of wolf
bites or clawing, but due to the accident. "Now let me the fuck in!" he
ordered, and he was granted admittance—then cleared by the mirror
checks inside the lift.

Once he was inside, he reported that all the troops—not just from
that base, but everyone who had answered the call to arms—had been
slaughtered. "They *knew* we were coming. And it's all down to that
parasite, Daniels!" When Grice, after rejecting medical assistance,
demanded that the youth be brought to him, it was discovered that
he'd overcome his guards and escaped.

"He didn't hurt us," offered Trooper Willis.

"Said he had something to do," reported Barnes.

"I'll bet he did! I want this entire facility on lockdown. I want the whole base searched." Not an inconsiderable feat for the handful of people who were left inside it. "Everywhere, look everywhere! I want that traitorous bastard found. And when he is, I'm going to—"

"You're going to do what?" Tommy Daniels had said, appearing behind him.

The men surrounding Grice raised their rifles, training them at the newcomer—but he was too close to their leader to fire (even if they'd wanted to). The General spun, hesitated for a second or so, then raised his finger and was jabbing it in Tommy's direction. "This is down to you, isn't it? You were the only other person it could have been. You practically admitted it to me before you attacked me! You can't even deny it, can you?"

Tommy spoke through gritted teeth. "I was trying to *warn* you!"

"All that blood is on your hands, Daniels! Your friend Ridgeway, all of them!"

The younger man looked down sadly.

"You'll pay for this, you really will!"

"I've paid all right," came Tommy's reply, holding Grice's gaze again. "But you're going to have bigger problems than me on your hands soon."

As if on cue, a soldier carrying a tablet came running up, shouting: "Sir! Sir . . . You're going to want to see this!"

"What is it?"

"The view from outside, a live feed." He handed the tablet to his superior officer, who sucked in a breath. The screen was split into four, CCTV cameras covering the whole of the area beyond the cave: in each direction. It looked at first glance like the ground was undulating, rippling even; just like it had done after the underground explosion. But that was only because there wasn't a single patch of ground that wasn't occupied, wasn't covered in fur. In things wearing that fur. And eyes, lots and lots of red eyes. The wolves Grice had gone in search of, the ones he believed to be hiding out at the zoo—their version of 1A—had come to him. Had most likely even followed him back. "It . . . it can't . . . They . . ." He looked at Tommy again. "This is your doing, isn't it?"

Tommy shook his head.

"It . . . They can't get in. We're safe enough in here," declared Grice, and even as he did so one of their number at the back—a creature with a silver streak to differentiate it from the rest—roared some kind of order. It was obviously Grice's opposite number. Suddenly a wall of the creatures rushed the rocks; rushed the exact place where the projection was, as if they knew they could get inside. Guns mounted there opened fire, silver bullet after silver bullet. Some of the wolves were mown down, only to be trampled by their brethren in their haste to get into the cave itself. The guns continued to fire, pumping out more ammunition—until they were ripped from the rocks by the beasts, or simply sliced to pieces by their claws. The end result was the same, that first line of defence was gone now—leaving nothing standing between the wolves and the lift down into 1A.

Grice pressed a button on the screen and the cameras switched to inside the cave itself now. He watched, open-mouthed as the tunnel there filled with the creatures. And then they were at the lift doors.

"They . . . they won't be able to get through those," said Grice, but his voice was wavering, sweat mixing with the blood at his forehead and dripping from it. "Even if they do, they—"

He'd stopped because they'd opened the doors of the lift. The sheer weight of numbers, the sheer amount of brute strength and clawing at the metal, had weakened them enough that they just popped apart. The lift itself was still down where they were, so at least it hadn't been made easy for them. They had quite a climb down, those beasts, but they were coming.

They were coming for them.

"We need to set up defensive positions at the corridor where the lift doors are," said Tommy. "Slow down their access to—"

"*You!*" Grice rounded on him. "You need to shut the fuck up! This is all on you!" He threw down the tablet he'd been holding, snatched a rifle from one of the soldiers standing nearby.

"None of this is *on* me," Tommy stated flatly. "I didn't ask for any of it."

It was Grice's turn to grit his teeth now, as he levelled the rifle at Tommy's head. "You've been a thorn in my side for far too long now. Time to end this."

Tommy was too quick for him, though: his reflexes astonishing. Even as Grice's finger was twitching on the trigger, he'd reached out and shoved the rifle into the air—so that when it went off, the bullets just hit the ceiling. Then he wrenched the gun out of Grice's hands, and turned it on his commanding officer. Grice let out a faint whine.

It looked to those present as if Tommy was going to return the favour. Just shoot Grice in cold blood, in the head. But then he brought the butt of the rifle up and struck the general on the temple. The man went down like he'd just been deflated.

Their leader lay there on the floor, wincing and moaning. When he looked up again, looked around at the soldiers gathered, he whimpered: "Are . . . are you just going to stand there? This is what he's wanted all along, to take charge!"

Tommy shook his head again. "That's the last thing I've ever wanted."

"He's going to get you all killed," argued Grice, touching his new wound and screwing up his face again.

"I'm trying to help!"

"Are you really going to listen to *him*?" Grice's voice was getting stronger by the minute. "Are you?"

"I will," came a voice from the back, from behind the ring of soldiers.

"W-Who . . . who are you?" Grice looked around, confused. "Who *is* that?"

"My name," said the man, stepping forwards, "is Trooper Andrew Southland from outpost 5C. They call me Angel. And this man saved my life. I thought I was as good as dead, those monsters everywhere I looked—but he got me out of that situation. I'm alive because of him. So, yes, I'll listen to Tommy Daniels. I'll follow him. I'd follow him into Hell, in fact . . . no disrespect, *sir*."

There was silence then, as the other soldiers present all looked at each other—including Barnes and Willis. And it was the latter who spoke next, saying: "What do you want us to do, Tommy?"

The lad nodded his thanks, to both Angel and Willis for their support. "We have to bottleneck them at the lift. Because if they get into the facility proper, you won't need to follow me to Hell.

"They'll be bringing it with them," he said finally.

℘

They were coming down the lift-shaft.

She could sense them, feel them. They were all over the rocks, like ants swarming over a hill—and now they were burrowing their way inside. To get to them all, to get to *her*. Coming down the lift.

No, coming up the lift: coming to the cave. Back where it all began.

Rachael shook her head again, trying to focus. But they were coming, so many of them. No: just one. The only one she had to worry about, coming up from where she'd buried him.

She'd told her son that she'd buy them all some time. Told him when he came down here demanding answers. Painful answers to questions he should never have had to ask. Should never have needed to ask his mother. Secrets that were no longer secrets, lies—or the omission of truths, which amounted to the same thing. But there was no hiding it any longer, there hadn't been when he'd burst in and seen the hair, the fur that was growing on her arms, her face. The tinge of red to her eyes, all of it reflected off the many mirrors in her room. As soon as she'd seen him, Rachael—was that who she still was? she forgot these days—had snapped back to her normal appearance. Too late . . . he'd seen it all. There was no more running away from it.

Someone had told him anyway, putting memories and thoughts into his head. They could do that if they wanted to, because of his link to her . . . to them all. Half-human, half . . . They'd pre-empted her, because she was going to tell him. Had been wanting to tell him, but just how do you broach that subject? Just how do you sit down with a cup of tea and tell your son that—

She'd run away from it herself for so long, not wanting to confront it. Pretending it had all been some kind of nightmare, that she'd imagined it. But if keeping one step ahead of the authorities hadn't been proof enough, there were the dreams. Rachael couldn't control those, and he'd come to her in them. That bastard Finch, reaching her when she was at her most relaxed, her most vulnerable. She'd always wake up in a cold sweat, of course, before anything happened. And remember him: Tommy. Why she was doing this, why she had to be strong.

It was a lonely life, no family left. No hope of any kind of relationship, not that anyone could compare to him . . . Tom. The love of her life. She had to give Finch that; if it hadn't been for him, she'd never have experienced that one night with Tom when her son had been conceived (she'd given up trying to work out the biology of that ages ago). Because actually she was—

Dead. Eaten.

But then if Finch hadn't come along maybe they would have had a chance at longer lasting happiness? A normal life, whatever that was. Just two normal human beings.

Maybe if she'd gone to him in the pub that night when she'd first seen him. But even then, the only reason he'd been there was because he was tracking the beast. Hunting Finch. With a team in tow, no less—had been doing it for years. So, even if the wolf hadn't targeted Rachael, that wouldn't have been an ordinary life. He wouldn't have given up putting those creatures down for her. Wouldn't have been able to. Tom's destiny had been decided a long time before he came to her city.

None of that mattered when her son had been standing in front of her. All that mattered was to be strong once more.

"Tommy," she'd begun, but he'd turned away; couldn't bear to look at her. Couldn't bear the knowledge of what she was. What, in turn, that made him. Heir to the throne. The king is dead (or is he?), long live the king! But there had always been much more of his father in him than . . . than his other father. Tommy was human, first and foremost. Not half anything, but maybe he could be a bridge? Maybe through him there could be some sort of peace?

No. They didn't want peace. They wanted chaos. They wanted this world, and they'd almost succeeded in getting it. Those reflections of *him*. Wanted their leader back, as well. Were coming to ensure that happened.

"Tommy," she'd repeated.

"Was it you?" he asked, still not looking up.

"Was . . ." But she knew what he was asking, felt it through those shared emotions. Had she been the one to betray humanity? She couldn't answer that, couldn't remember. In a dream maybe?

"Or did I do it?" He was staring right at her then, and she wished that he wasn't. An accusatory gaze, bitter and resentful.

"I-I don't . . . Tommy, you . . . you have to listen to me. They're coming. You have to stop them from . . . They mustn't reach me in here." It was what they'd wanted all along. Why they'd been looking for her, for Tommy. It was also why she'd shut herself away in the deepest, darkest hole she could find when everything crumbled to dust. Where she couldn't even feel them, sense them; and vice versa. Wasn't only the authorities she'd been avoiding all this time. Now they knew exactly where she was; they'd read her son, and he'd told her.

"How am I supposed to stop them?" he asked her. "For Heaven's sake, how do I know they won't just take me over?"

"They won't . . . they *can't* do that. You're too strong, Tommy. You always have been. Like *I* used to be." She sighed. "Like I have to be again." She needed to be strong, just for a little while longer. Until this was over once and for all. "I-I beat him once, I can . . . can do it again."

"Can you? *Can* you, though?"

"I can do my best," she promised him. "I can buy you some time. But you have to buy me some." Rachael attempted a smile. No more running, it was time to stand and fight. "You have your battle to face. I have mine." The struggle to remain focused, to convince him that she was in charge, was tremendous. Especially after the state she'd been in recently (Christ, she'd even attacked him the last time he'd visited!), especially after what he'd seen when he flung open that door. "I'm sorry," she managed. "Really sorry for everything, son."

He shook his head. "It wasn't your fault," he told her. "But you should have told me. Should have told me *everything*."

"I know." Neither of them said anything for a short while that seemed to last a lifetime. "Tommy, you have to go. They're close now. *Please!*"

"Right," he said.

"I-I really do love you, you know. More than anything."

"I . . ." He paused, then came over to where she was sitting, where she was always sitting. Tommy came over and gave her the biggest hug he'd ever given her, then kissed her cheek. "I love you too, Mum."

Then he was gone, and the pain of loss competed with that of the forces vying for attention inside her. She could see them, not in the woods anymore. Not out on the streets, but up there, outside this base. Approaching the rocks that marked out where they were hidden.

Not only that, but *she* was with them. That made Rachael suck in a sharp breath, the sight of her like that. What had been done to her. She was leading them across the land, then hung back when they reached the actual base. The wolf with the silver streak. The one she recognised.

The one who'd ordered them to rush the cave, then the tunnel inside. To brave the guns and reach the lift.

"Oh no . . . What have you done?" she whispered.

The doors to the lifts were open, and they were inside—clambering downwards, getting closer.

While he was in her head, rising. In the lift to reach the cave, a mixture of the original one and this.

Wolves coming down, one wolf—*the* wolf—coming up (she could hear him, oh God, she could hear him!)

And the fate of absolutely everything hanging in the balance.

෴

153

They were in position.

In the corridor where the lifts normally opened, to go through the checking process. Soldiers on the floor, rifles pointed up at the lift doors; others standing, targeting them from a higher position. Waiting for the mutts to break through, waiting to pick them off as they entered the space.

The young lad next to Andrew 'Angel' Southland was shaking so much you could practically hear his teeth chattering. "First time in a firefight?" Angel asked him, and the boy nodded. "What's your name?"

"Eddie . . . Eddie Haines."

"Okay, Eddie. Well, the good news is they can't come at us all at once . . . or surround us. And we're only the secondary line of defence, because we have those." He pointed to the cannons on the wall; not that similar mounted guns had done any good up above. "So, we have the upper hand in that respect. But pick your targets, make every shot count." It was his fallback advice, the same advice he'd given the survivors on the bus. "Breathe, and take your time."

"You . . . you've done this before?"

Angel laughed. "I've been in a similar predicament, yeah. Believe it or not, though, this time I think we stand a better chance."

"W-What happened back then? You know, the other time?"

"*He* happened," Angel gestured back towards Tommy Daniels. "Him and his men. They found us, rescued us."

"N-Nobody's coming to find us this time, are they?"

Angel seemed to think about this, then clapped the lad on the shoulder. "You just make every one of those shots count, all right?"

Eddie nodded, so hard it looked like his head was going to come off.

Then the noise, the banging. Everyone froze; even Eddie stopped shaking.

They'd broken into the lift itself, probably through the roof, and were trying to open the doors the same as they had up above. Gain access to 1A.

"Okay, get ready people." This was from Tommy. "They're coming!" If they hadn't known it before, there was the unmistakable growling echoing up the corridor. The sound of claws on metal. Then the lights went out, turned red—which made it look more like Hell than ever—and an alarm started up.

Suddenly they weren't just coming anymore.

They were inside.

They were here.

CHAPTER TWELVE

SHE'D BUMPED INTO THEM BOTH IN THE CORRIDOR, ON HER WAY TO Peel's quarters.

Before that, she'd been thinking about what to do, tucked away in one of her cubby holes where she went when she needed to get her head straight: a storage room really that hardly anyone used. A quiet place to go when she needed to make a decision. Should she go to Peel with this, see what he had to say about it? What he made of the situation with Tommy? Would that get him into even more trouble than he was obviously in?

But what was the alternative, go to Grice? That would definitely land Tommy in the shit, given it had been on that man's orders he'd been locked away in his room in the first place.

It had been while she'd been pondering all of this that she'd started, woken up when the alarms had begun going off. She hadn't even realised she was so tired, but then the last few days had been pretty rough; and she'd lost that blood when she'd offered herself up as bait.

Then the lights went out, before turning scarlet.

Pat knew what that meant, the same as everyone else in this place: a breach. Now she knew exactly where she should be, her mind made up for her.

She needed to get to Peel.

She'd pelted down one corridor, up another, heading for his quarters. The temporary quarters they'd given him anyway; it was anybody's guess whether he'd remain there. Whether he was going to stay here for good. Then again, if there had been a breach, an actual honest to goodness breach, then how long would any of them be able to stay?

Or even stay alive?

She'd rounded the corner that would take her to his room when she'd almost run into them both, skidding to a halt so she didn't fall over them. Peel and the doc. Together. It threw her momentarily, seeing them like that—seeing that they'd quite clearly come from his place. She wasn't quite sure how she felt about it. At once excited, happy and a little wary . . . not that she had any right to be anything at all. Or did she, given that she loved both of these people?

That's right, she thought to herself: I *love* them, like family. Stuff to deal with, to work through another time . . .

Dr Kingsley had been telling Peel about the alarms, the lighting, about what it meant and he was asking her where the weapons were kept. Specifically where his confiscated axe could be found.

The pair of them were just as surprised to see Pat. "You okay?" was the first thing Peel asked her.

"Yeah. I was coming to find you," she said, looking from him to the doctor.

"Good. That's good . . . You're probably going to need a weapon as well, just to be on the safe side."

"We'll swing by the armoury on the way up," Kinglsey said. "What? I'm not going to be the odd one out, and I know my way around a gun."

"Of course you do . . . Major," said Peel, smirking. The kind of smirk only people who've shared some kind of intimacy could pull off. Something had definitely happened between those two—and after everything he'd said about Tommy! Stuff to deal with later, Pat said again to herself. If there was a later.

As they followed Dr Kingsley, Peel leaned over and said: "I need to talk to you."

"What about?" asked Pat.

"Hold on, why were you looking for me again?"

Pat nodded at him, insisting: "You first."

"Okay," he said, keeping his voice low. "I've just found out who your boyfriend is."

Pat couldn't help it, she screwed up her face. "Tommy? He's *not* my boyfriend."

"You know what I mean. You'd like him to be."

"I don't think that . . ." She paused. "What do you mean you've found out who he is?"

"Daniels," stated Peel. "It can't be a coincidence."

"What can't? You're not making any sense."

She could see that he realised there were whole chunks of this Pat didn't know, that he needed to get her up to speed on. But, for now, he just said: "The woman I saved, back at that motel."

Pat nodded. "What about it?"

"I think . . . well, I think it might have been Tommy's mother. And I think the dead guy, the one who was killed by the wolf, might have been his dad. The timing fits if nothing else."

"Just because he's called Daniels?"

Peel shook his head. "He looks like him! I couldn't put my finger on it at first, but he's a real mix of the two of them."

"Okay, so . . . I'm still not sure I follow you. You saved his mum; that's a good thing, isn't it?"

He said nothing for a moment or two, just kept marching after Dr Kingsley, then suddenly: "She knew about The First Wolf, Pat."

"What?"

"His mother, Rachael. It was in the psychiatric reports, the ones before she did a runner. They were a lot easier to get hold of once all the shit hit the fan and folk were running about like headless chickens. I wanted . . . I *needed* to know whether there was some kind of conspiracy going on, whether the powers that be knew about the shapeshifters."

Pat was racing to catch up, both figuratively and literally as Peel tried to match the pace of the doctor. "I still don't see—"

He glanced back at her. "I've been looking for her all these years, figured she'd gone into hiding or something. Deep undercover. Or she died, was killed by another of those things. Either way, Tommy would probably know. And she might have passed something on to him. Vital information about them. Certainly explains why he's so good at what he does, why he's got such a rep."

"But—"

"You should have read some of the stuff his mother was coming out with, Pat. Dreams about them, all sorts. I keep asking myself how she knew about The First Wolf, unless she encountered it? Maybe that's why she was on the run with Tommy's dad in the first place? Maybe it was after her? In any event, it wasn't the one I killed when I saved her, that's for sure."

"How do you know that?" she asked.

"Nothing changed. Didn't stop anything. In fact it only got worse." Another shake of the head. "No, that big bastard's still out there somewhere, and this is the first real clue I've had in ages about it."

"Doesn't do us much good though if we're trapped down here, if the hounds have finally found us." Pat waved her hand around to indicate the colour of the lights, the alarm that was still going; 1A on high alert.

"I still need to talk to Tommy. The doc said that he'd been locked up somewhere?" Peel looked at his companion, to see if she knew that as well. Probably figuring there was a good chance she did.

"He's . . ." began Pat. "Listen, that's what I wanted to talk to you about."

"I'm all ears," Peel replied.

"Tommy broke out," she told him.

"Of confinement?" Peel grinned at that, a look of admiration she thought. "Like mother like son, eh? How do you know?"

"I . . . I was sort of waiting for him, waiting to talk to him when he was let out. Because, well, because of . . . y'know."

"I do. And I owe you an apology about that."

That was nice, that felt good. All this going on around them, what could be an incursion into their camp by the dogs, and Peel's apology seemed like the most important thing in the world. "I'm . . . I'm sorry too," she said.

"So, where is he now?"

"I kind of followed him."

Another smirk from Peel.

"I'm not a crazy stalker person or anything."

"Course not." He grinned again.

She shrugged. "Anyway, he went down into like the bowels of this place. I've never even been there before, and he's never mentioned it but . . . I followed him to this room, this corridor with a door at the end of it. He went inside."

"What's in there?"

Pat shrugged again. "I only got a peek, but it looked like there were mirrors in there. *Lots* of mirrors. And . . . and, well, I thought I saw someone."

"Someone?" Peel looked as confused as she'd been moments before.

"I don't know, I just . . . I overhear things sometimes, stupid rumours. About food being taken to someone, a VIP or whatever. Nobody really knows much though, it's like a . . . Like you said, a legend. More of a myth than anything."

"And Tommy was there, today?" She could see the cogs going round in Peel's mind. What he was thinking: that if Tommy was here, and someone really was in that room . . .

"I can take you there, when we know what's going on." She'd said it before she had a chance to think about the words. Wouldn't that be a betrayal of her loyalty to Tommy? But then what of her loyalty to Peel? An impossible choice to make. And didn't she want to know herself what was down there, what Tommy was keeping from her? His biggest secret.

"Sounds like a plan," Peel said and the grin became a warm smile.

"What are you two whispering about back there?" asked Dr Kingsley, in the self-conscious way people do when they think they're the one being discussed.

"Nothing," answered Peel, which would probably do little to dismiss those concerns.

"Hmm. Anyway, we're here." She was opening a storage room with a key-card. "Fill your boots, guys."

Pat watched as Peel moved past them both, zeroing straight in on one weapon in particular. "There she is," he said, hefting the axe. "That other lady in my life."

She exchanged a look with Dr Kingsley then, and they both shook their heads at the same time.

"What?" said Peel, and grinned like a schoolboy again.

ↄ

They didn't have to go much further before they heard the sound of battle: machine-gun fire and shouting.

Screaming.

They'd been waiting for Peel to finish grabbing stuff from the armoury, which including filling a bag he slung over one shoulder. "Used to be in the Boy Scouts when I was little. Always be prepared for anything, right?" he'd said with a wink as they stood there urging him to get a move on.

Dr Kingsley had plumped for a serious-looking assault rifle, with a couple of handguns in holsters on either side of her hips. Pat had turned over gun after gun in her hands, trying to decide which one to go for, when Peel had pointed her in the direction of one of the simplest. "You just point and shoot," he told her, trying to be helpful she knew, but she'd taken it as babying once more.

"I *know*. I take them on missions," Pat reminded him. She didn't tell Peel she hated the things, nor that she hoped against hope she wouldn't need to use it. None of them knew the size of the attack; could just have been a single wolf who'd somehow penetrated their defences; might have been a handful.

But in spite of what Peel had said, nobody had been prepared for what they faced. What they encountered as they rushed through the canteen section of the base. At first, it had only been a lone figure stumbling through—retreating. Covered in blood, staggering against tables and chairs, Pat still recognised their commanding officer: Grice. He was waving a pistol around in the air: waving it around everywhere in fact. Including at them occasionally, which prompted Peel try and put himself between them and the injured man.

But Dr Kingsley was having none of it, pushing past and shouting: "General!"

He stared at the other people in the room, as if seeing them for the first time. "Doctor . . . Dr Kingsley, is that you?"

"Yes," she replied, "of course! Who else would it be?" But then, if there had been a break-in, she could be one of those things—because they could be anybody, thought Pat. Could even be the general? He squinted, but seemed to take her at her word. "You're wounded. What's going on?"

Grice looked down at himself, at the blood. "This, oh this is nothing. Tip of the iceberg. Didn't even happen . . . It happened out there! They . . . Dr Kingsley, they killed them all!"

"What?"

"We were supposed to . . . But they knew we were coming. Daniels, he knew that they knew." It was beginning to sound farcical. They knew that we knew that they knew. Nobody was laughing, though.

"How do you mean, Tommy knew?" Pat was suddenly asking him, her commanding officer, who she'd barely spoken to in all her time here at 1A.

"Their plans!" the general spat. "I think he . . . He must be working with them!"

"Tommy Daniels?" Even Dr Kingsley had trouble believing that one. After all the lives he'd saved, all the wolves he'd taken down.

In spite of this, the general nodded emphatically. "Working with them somehow, I don't know . . . But they're all dead! Everyone! And now, now those men back there . . . They wouldn't listen, they're going to die too. Those . . . those things are going to get in. *Are* in!"

"How many are—" Peel began to ask, but then soldiers entered the room from the far side, walking backwards and firing ahead of them. Holding something off, shapes in the corridor they'd just come from. Bundles of fur.

And suddenly they were in the canteen: wolves. Pat counted three, four . . . then there were a dozen or more. "Oh fuck!" shouted Grice, though it was more of a wail really. He bolted sideways, attempting to escape—but a mutt spotted him, bounded after the running figure.

Grice fired back a few times, but again wasn't really aiming properly and the bullets went wide. Then the creature jumped up on a table, dived for him, landing on his back and sending him sprawling into more tables and chairs. It sat on him, pinning the man to the ground, biting into him at the neck and tearing away great chunks of flesh, before lapping up the blood. And just as suddenly the animal was being peppered with bullets, Dr Kingsley striding towards it and firing: every single one of her bullets finding their target. It looked like it was dancing for a second, then it slumped over and fell into a corner. The doctor ejected her magazine, reached into the jacket of her white coat and slammed another one home.

"I think I'm in love," Pat heard Peel say under his breath, then to her: "Stay down." The next thing she knew he was wading into the action himself, axe swinging left and right, biting into those things himself with his blade.

Pat gasped at what was happening in front of her, the soldiers trying to hold back the tide of wolves streaming through into the canteen. She took Peel's advice and got down low, but one had already seen her and was heading her way. Pat scrambled under a table just as the dog reached her, jumping onto the table itself and causing the legs to buckle.

She looked around desperately for Peel, but couldn't see him. Couldn't rely on his help. Shouldn't have to, she reminded herself—but then the wolf's mouth came down between tables, jaws snapping, and she let out a cry of panic.

Fight or flight? Definitely fight . . .

The gun! Almost an afterthought, but she remembered it. Remembered Peel's words about pointing and shooting. She brought it up, pulling the trigger, catching the beast in the shoulder, but only making it angrier.

"Shit!" Pat scrabbled sideways, only just avoiding a claw that came down to her right. She fired upwards again, but this time the gun was knocked out of her hands and clattered uselessly onto the floor. *Your cross*, she thought then. But even as she was reaching around her neck for it, the wolf was bearing down. Pat pulled it off, swung it around. However the mutt simply grabbed it, ignoring the smoke that was coming from its paw as it held the silver, wrenching it from her grasp and flinging it away.

The chain and cross, the present her mum had given her so long ago. Her dead mum—killed by these things, like so many others had been. Pat let out a growl of anger herself, rising and lifting the side of the table. Destabilising her enemy, causing it to lose its balance and pitch backwards. It wouldn't stay there for long, though; she had to think of something and fast. There was a chair nearby, so she got hold of that, bringing the leg down and jamming it into the wolf's chest. Wasn't silver, as far as she knew. Wouldn't kill it . . . but it would keep it down while she—

There! Pat rolled and snatched up the gun she'd lost, then got close enough again that she couldn't possibly miss. The silver bullet entered the beast's temple, blowing its brains out the other side. It shuddered once, twice, then stopped moving. She sat back, panting for breath. When she looked up again, she saw wolf bodies everywhere—in pieces mainly, so figured it was probably Peel's handiwork. He'd cleared the field for the time being at least. He and Dr Kingsley were rounding up the soldiers that were left, bringing them back into a more defensive position. Upturning tables so they could shoot from behind them. An attempt to stem the flow of more monsters into the canteen.

Peel eventually joined her, looking down at her fresh kill. "Nice work," he said.

"Thanks."

"And I believe this is yours?" He held out the chain and cross, handed it to her. She had no clue when he'd picked it up.

Beaming, she repeated her thanks. "Is Grice. . .?"

He nodded. "You're looking at the new commanding officer of 1A." For a moment or two she thought Peel meant himself. But when she followed his gaze, and Pat saw the woman barking out orders, organising the troops, she knew he meant Dr Kingsley. *Major* Kingsley. She saw the look in Peel's eyes as well, the pride and admiration. When he'd said he was in love, he really hadn't been kidding.

Which reminded her: "Has anyone seen Tommy, do you know?" With a bit of luck he was still deep inside this place, away from everything and safe.

Now Peel looked down.

"What?" Pat grabbed his sleeve, demanded to know what he did.

He thumbed back. "A few of the men just came from the entrance. He was with them there."

"So where is he now?" Pat tried to keep her voice from rising, but couldn't.

"He was holding them off, buying them some time to retreat," Peel explained.

But there had been wolves in the canteen, which meant they'd got past him. Which meant that . . . No, he wasn't dead. He *couldn't* be dead.

As if reading her thoughts, Peel said: "I'm sure he's all right. If nothing else, I've seen that Tommy can look after himself."

Pat thought briefly about rushing off towards that entrance where the soldiers had appeared, rushing to try and help Tommy. But already more of the brutes were appearing and the air was filled with gunfire once more. She nodded, taking in what Peel had said: "I'm sure he's all right."

But not knowing whether to believe it herself.

CHAPTER THIRTEEN

BLACKNESS.

That's all he'd known for the longest time. Now he was rising out of it. Heading towards the light. Heading for freedom. For consciousness . . . How long had he been out of it? He had no idea. He could remember bits and pieces from before he went under, from before the darkness claimed him. A bright light, a loud noise.

Then *bam!*

Nothing. Nada.

He'd been doing something before, had been in the middle of something. Attacking someone. Yes, that was it. Attacking . . . No, fighting. Was that the same thing? *Being* attacked. That's right. That's how he'd lost his grip on reality.

He'd been hit by something. Remembered flying through the air to land . . . That's when he'd struck his head. That's when everything had gone black.

But he had to wake up now, get back to his life. Come on, open your eyes dammit! Might be dead? Was he dead? Had they killed him? And who were *they*?

It came back to him in flashes: fur; teeth; claws.

Wolves.

That's what he'd been doing! That's what he and his men had been doing. In the corridor, the lift corridor. Yes, that was it.

They'd held them off as long as possible. The mounted cannons blazed above their heads, the bullets from rifles and handguns finding their marks. But there had simply been too many in the end, coming through the top of the lift, down the lift-shaft itself to claw their way into 1A. And then they'd taken out those wall guns by hurling chunks of the lift at them, smashing them. One had even fallen on a trooper below who was laying on the floor firing upwards at them. Smitty his name had been . . . before the cannon had crushed him.

His men had at least been targeting the wolves, headshots mostly but anything that would just incapacitate them. It was becoming increasingly clear, though, that the sheer weight of numbers would win the day. That's when he'd ordered them to fall back from the corridor.

"Angel, lead them away from this," he'd said, looking from that man to Eddie Haines who looked like he was on the verge of breaking down. "They'll follow you now."

"And what are you going to do?" Angel had asked.

"I still have a few tricks up my sleeve," had been his reply, clapping Angel on the shoulder and telling him: "Now go!"

As the troops from the corridor retreated, covering each other, he'd brought out his walkie-talkie and depressed the button. "Deepak, it's time to bring out the big guns!"

Then a door was opening off to the side of the corridor, the one newcomers to the base usually had to go through to be tested. This time, instead, someone came out of it. Someone holding a very big gun indeed.

"Concentrate your fire up the middle," he told his gunner, who crouched and hefted the weapon onto his shoulder, then pressed the trigger. The rocket flew from the bazooka, flew straight up the corridor and into the new grouping of mutts emerging. The blast scattered them in every direction, blood and internal organs painting the walls.

Smoke filled the corridor, which Deepak wafted away. By the time it had cleared, a wolf was springing in his direction—leaping on him and savaging the soldier before he could load again.

"*No!*" Tommy cried.

The smoke was thinning out, showing more dogs pushing their way through the lift doors and inside. There was a never-ending supply apparently, and all that stood between them and making it into the base proper was him.

He ran to meet them, drawing his pistol and firing; taking down one, two, four, six . . . Until he was empty, and had to resort to his knife—bringing that up and under the chin of one beast, punching another on the snout that was coming to help its kin. Ordinarily, that would have had little effect at all—they barely felt blows from human beings, they were simply too strong. But this caused it to pull back, pause, cock its head. Perhaps it was the sheer audacity of one of his kind trying to go toe-to-toe with one of theirs . . .

Or was it something else?

In any event, that hesitation cost it dearly. "For Deepak!" he said, and jammed the still-bloody knife sideways into thing's ear.

The advance had halted momentarily when he looked up. The wolves ahead of him stopping and staring. Just like they had done in the park that time; only a few days ago, but it felt like years. And he had to ask himself then, had any of them ever really tried to kill him? Ever come close?

He stared back, breathing hard, focus shifting from one pair of eyes to the next (red, he knew, but then everything was at the moment because of the lights). Almost willing them to do *something*.

Moments later, he wished that he hadn't. It was like the PLAY button had been pressed and they were suddenly surging forwards once more. His knife slashed left and right, but it barely slowed any of them down. And soon he was being barrelled into, carried along—carried out through the main door again at the end of the corridor, then thrown into the wall.

Thrown clear, as a matter of fact.

His last memory before the darkness was of a procession of fur marching past. Marching to war with the last vestiges of humanity. About to wipe out all resistance.

Then his eyes were closing and he was blacking out.

But now he was rising from that blackness. Rising up and remembering what he had to do. The mission he must carry on with, no matter what the cost. He could feel his battered body, was willing something else entirely. For it to move, for command over it once more.

That was when Tommy Daniels finally opened his eyes again.

&

She'd seen it all.

Not just through her own eyes, but through *theirs*. Keeping well back, as a good leader should, directing her troops. Giving them silent commands, both individually and as a whole.

The creature with the silver streak of fur. The monster who had once been human such a long time ago. Who had once been so weak, but now was stronger than she ever could have imagined. She had memories of her former life, of course she did. Mainly the pain, frustration . . . the indignity. Brought about by people like—

Rachael. Rachael Daniels.

The girl who had started all this in the first place. The girl who had kept their master imprisoned all this time, and would pay for what she had done.

No, hadn't there been kindness? Hadn't she tried to help, tried to *save*—

That didn't matter now, not after all this. It had begun with them, and it would end with them as well.

And the end was almost here. Most of what was left of the resistance had been wiped out in the explosion at the zoo. Quite a clever trick to turn their own plans against them, thanks to a little insider information. Now, they were at the humans' final base; turning things around on them again. Would take back what was theirs: the cave, their king. To rule, finally to rule—with her at his right-hand side.

Consequently, they'd marched on the rocks, they'd broken down their automatic defences, and were in the process of gaining access to the facility. Did she feel sorry for the wolves who had given their lives for this? Not really, they'd done so gladly. Cannon fodder were a part of any battle or war (her father, who had been in the army, who had fought at Rorke's Drift ironically, had taught her that). Without their sacrifice, they wouldn't have been able to get inside. They'd be remembered when all this was over, honoured.

Those who were still giving their lives below in that corridor, as she sent squadron after squadron down the shaft—clawing their way quickly downwards, filling that hallway and eventually filling the base itself. They'd braved the mounted guns, the minimal force waiting for them; even the projectile fired as a last-ditch attempt to slow things down. Had driven it all back. Then—

Him. The boy.

Standing in the corridor, killing their kind. The way he'd gazed at them each in turn, it had actually sent a shiver down her spine. He shouldn't even exist, and yet he did. If their master was the king, then this was his prince, she supposed. His offspring . . . not that he saw it that way. Fought rather than embraced his destiny, while they weren't allowed to harm a hair on his head.

Still, he wasn't their primary objective that day—and nobody had said anything about not knocking him out. Putting him out of the game until it was won. So that's what she'd done, ordering more and more of her troops into the shaft, into the corridor. Up other corridors, into more and more parts of the base. Chasing all the stragglers and eliminating them, no matter how hard they resisted. It would be a slower process than she would've preferred, but filling a receptacle had to start with the first drops of liquid. Filling—

The kettle . . . Having a nice cup of tea with . . .

"Things are catching up with me, dear. Time, for one."

She shook her head. Needed to concentrate, today of all days. Soon this would all be over, one way or another. He was rising, and they would be there to meet him when he arrived.

℘

He was rising, out of the blackness.

Out of the dark. That's all he'd known for the longest time, but not anymore. Trapped inside that bitch's cage. Inside her head, as she waltzed around in his body! The indignity of it. Oh, he had such plans for her. He'd make her suffer. He'd bury her deep, deep inside where she'd put him. Make her witness everything, make her endure what was to come.

Before, he'd only been able to creep out in her dreams—and even then only for short periods of time. Chinks of freedom, but he'd taken them. Working on her until, eventually, she'd begun to question her very sanity. Causing her to lose her grip on reality. And as she'd gotten weaker, he'd become stronger. Until, finally, he was now strong enough to break free completely. To take back what was his. What belonged to him.

Plans within plans, not so secret secrets. Games. He shivered with the delight at the thought of it, the man who'd once been William Oliver Finch. Who'd once crawled into that cave to get out of the cold, hungry and delirious. Who'd defeated and eaten the wolf he'd encountered in there, only to take on its characteristics. Its bloodlust and appetites.

Oh, how he'd make her pay—make her suffer!

Then there was the boy: the freak he'd watched being born, who'd come out of his own body . . . Was he a blessing or a curse? Would he join them, or have to be destroyed? Finch's heir or his mortal enemy? He was not to be harmed until that was determined. If it turned out he was the latter, just a walking, talking reminder of his weakness—his years of captivity—he'd force his jailer to watch the lad's demise. He could think of no greater torture than that for her.

The lift was ascending. The lift she was picturing in her mind now, containing him. Drawing Finch up to face her once more. This time things would go very differently, he wouldn't pull his punches in any way, shape or form.

"Rachael Daniels," he growled, licking his lips. "I'm coming for you."

He was rising, remembering, knew what he had to do—what he'd been in the middle of doing. Attacking . . . No, fighting. No, *being* attacked. But it was time to end all that.

Finch was ready and he'd almost arrived. It was time for the lift doors to open.

Time to open his eyes and shut out the blackness once and for all.

CHAPTER FOURTEEN

I T WAS LIKE THERE WAS A SEA, AND THEY WERE AN ISLAND IN THE middle of it.

As more and more of the creatures had entered the canteen, they'd encircled the remaining survivors—a dozen, if that—making it impossible to escape. Causing them to form a circle themselves, so they could see every angle as the enemy closed in. Covering fire had kept them mostly at bay so far, but it wouldn't hold them forever. And as Peel risked another look over the edge of an upturned table—one of several they were using for defence—the thought struck him about the ocean, that it was eroding the island bit by bit. Soon it would cover them completely and that would be the end of it.

One of the wolves butted the table he was next to, and Peel rose, swung his axe, and took out the immediate threat. It was all they could do, hold them off as long as possible. He glanced over at Kingsley . . . Andrea. He was so proud of the way she'd taken charge after Grice. But her command would be at an end before it had really begun if they didn't get out of there.

Pat too, shooting now through a gap in the tables. He was proud of her as well. Couldn't be prouder, in fact—not just of the way she was fighting, but the way she was coping with Tommy; with the knowledge of what had obviously happened to him near the entrance. The daughter Peel had never been blessed with, but had been given anyway. He knew she felt the same way. If they made it out of this—how? how were they going to make it out of this?—maybe they'd have a shot at being a family. Him, Kingsley and Pat. Dangerous thoughts; dangerous *dreams*, especially now.

Especially as the wolves were preparing to rush them from all sides. The soldier he knew as Eddie Haines, who'd appeared with another called Angel, were covering the rear of the circle. But if they chose to, Peel knew those mutts could batter them completely. After all, they'd forced their way inside a top secret military bunker; what could they do to stop them? Probably nothing, but they could take a few with them . . .

Peel's hand was reaching down, reaching for the bag he'd brought along and hoped he wouldn't have to use. Hoped also that the alarm—which had been cut off now, replaced by the howls and growls of the intruders—and the red lights only signified a small attack. One wolf, maybe a handful. Not this, not *all* of the fuckers!

His fingertips were almost brushing the contents when someone shouted: "Look! Good God . . . Look at that!"

Peel looked up and around, knew he'd probably regret it because it couldn't be anything good. Could it?

Could it?

To be honest, he couldn't really tell either way to begin with. The dogs had halted their approach, that much he could tell, and they'd ceased their growling, their snarling. They were practically silent, and the effect was genuinely disturbing.

"What are they playing at?" This was Kingsley, who'd joined him. "What are they waiting for?"

"Just be thankful they are," he replied, but there was more weirdness to come.

The wolves were separating, parting. Starting up at the far end, where the soldiers had appeared, there was a gap—and that gap was now ripping open the mass of fur. Peel and Kingsley watched as it proceeded up towards where their little 'camp' was. The wolves there stood back from each other, clearing a path . . . but for what?

Then they both saw it. Saw *him*. He was limping, his torso moving left and right, swivelling to face hounds on either side of the divide he was shuffling down. He still wore his cap and had a weapon, a silver knife, which he was threatening them with—but to Peel it didn't look like they were particularly scared of this, or indeed him. Why should they be? Because of the legend? The stories that he'd heard himself? No, it looked more like they were making way out of common courtesy or something.

"Pat," he called, "I think you're gonna want to see this."

She joined them both, as did the others in the circle, now that they didn't need to defend their positions. Gaping at the man treading this path down from the entrance towards them.

"Tommy," she whispered, like she could hardly believe he was there. Peel knew how she felt. Louder now: "But what—"

Peel put a finger to his lips to quieten her down again, as if it might break whatever spell had been put on the wolves.

Tommy continued his approach, warning the hounds with his knife: keeping the channel open. Then suddenly he'd reached the upturned tables, was beckoning the survivors to join him, turning and facing in the direction of the exit. Motioning for them to follow him as they made their way across to it. The escape they'd been hoping for.

"Do . . . do we go?" asked Eddie.

"You want to *stay*?" Peel replied, gathering up his things and catching the smile that passed between Pat and Tommy in the process. Relief that he was okay, or still alive anyway.

Kicking away the tables, they trailed Tommy as he cut another swathe through.

If I'm Noah, thought Peel, *then this guy is Moses, taking us to the other side of the Red Sea. Away from the island and—*

Someone was tugging on his arm and he looked over. It was Pat, nodding back in the direction Tommy had come from. The path there had folded in on itself, but rising above the other wolves—maybe being lifted higher than them—was a figure who stood out from, as well as above, the crowd.

The wolf with the silver streak in its fur.

"We need to hurry," he said, telling her to pass it down the line. Tommy speeded up and they followed, closely mirroring him, hoping that their luck would hold out until they could reach the exit.

Then suddenly the gap was closing behind them, and two troopers were being pulled into the mass; being 'drowned' in the sea. There was a crack of gunfire, and someone shouted "Run!"

No-one needed telling twice. The spell had been well and truly broken, possibly because of the presence of the older wolf. Peel swung his axe in an arc, lopping the mutts closest to pieces. Kingsley grabbed hold of Pat's arm and dragged her along, dragging her through the open door that Tommy was holding for them. Angel followed next, then Eddie. Then a female trooper Peel was pushing ahead of him, buying her some time to get through. But two more by his side were pulled into the throng, blood jetting upwards seconds later.

Peel dove through the doorway, aware of claws snatching at his legs and feet. Then the door was slammed behind him, the lock clicked in place. It wouldn't hold them for long—if at all. Perhaps till the next door along the hallway? But it was something. It was a chance.

Peel was aware of a hand sticking out in front of him to pull him to his feet. "Tommy," he said, accepting it gratefully, "when . . . *if* we get out of here, I think you and me need to have a conversation."

The lad in the cap said nothing, just urged them to keep on moving.

"Where are we going?" asked someone, Peel didn't catch who.

"We have no choice now, we have to go down," Tommy replied.

But as Kingsley, Pat, Angel, Eddie and the other remaining troopers went on ahead, they were all looking back. All trying to work out how they managed to get out of that.

All trying to work out exactly how Tommy Daniels had done what he'd done.

CHAPTER FIFTEEN

A s long as she could remember, Dr Andrea Kingsley, Major Andrea Kingsley, had spent as much time putting people back together again as she had taking them apart.

Dual roles, the soldier and the doctor. Both opposing one another, a battle raging inside of her, especially when she was in the combat zone. Of course, it was a sliding scale and the kind of combat she was currently engaged in made it easy. Seeing victims like the trooper at her feet, bleeding profusely from his wounds—having been sliced open at the gut—made it easy. Made her want to kill every last one of those hairy fucks back there, if she hadn't before. Made her want to make them suffer.

Eddie Haines couldn't have been more than what, nineteen? The sweetest kid tossed into this mess and expected to survive; he'd never really stood a chance, had he. Kingsley was trying to get his intestines to stay inside his stomach—using bandages she always carried about her person—and failing miserably. Knowing that the infection would already be coursing through his veins anyway. That if she didn't do what was necessary she'd be putting them all at risk.

Wasn't the first casualty either as they'd begun their descent, travelling lower and lower down stairways, fending off attacks as the mutts tracked them. Perilously low on ammo now, running out of places to go, to hide. Running out of options.

Running . . . hiding.

Eddie was just the latest, caught off guard when a wolf came through one of the doorways to the right—ripping through him like he was paper. Peel and Angel had taken care of the menace, but it had already been too late. For Trooper Eddie Haines, she thought, maybe it had started off too late and gone from there.

"Is he. . .?" This was Angel, crouching now with her.

"He's beginning to turn," she stated, trying to keep the emotion out of her voice. She was their leader now, for God's sake—she had to set an example. Couldn't afford to crumble on them. Kingsley looked up and over at Peel. She'd been trying to keep her emotions in check regarding that situation as well, ever since his quarters. Before that, even. When she'd heard he was gone, she'd felt that loss—and tried not to. Tried to keep it at arm's length. And when she knew he'd come back again, not only that but he'd survived some kind of crazy mission Tommy Daniels had dragged him along on, she'd felt relief and some kind of hope for a second chance. Hope that they might be together . . . and they had. Those hours had been the best of her life, but when he'd started saying all that stuff about her being special, beautiful . . . that's when the fear had kicked in again. The knee-jerk reaction to anyone getting close, getting inside. The same kind of protective armour she knew he had as well. Or she thought he'd had.

What a mess. That and what was happening here, right now, to Eddie Haines. Fucked up—the situation and what she'd done. Now more than ever, it wasn't the time to have feelings for someone, wasn't the time to . . . to fall in love with someone.

Shit!

Concentrate. She had a job to do, had to focus. What, like she had back in the canteen during that first fight? Taking charge of the men after Grice was killed, but with one eye on what Peel was doing; wondering whether he was safe or not. She needn't have worried, Kingsley had never seen anyone fight like he did. She felt pride . . . was she allowed to feel that? Was actually in awe of his skills, honed out there in the wilderness. Before that even, as a hunter putting down those wolves when hardly anyone knew about them.

"Doc . . . Doc?" Angel's voice brought her back to the here and now, forcing her to face up to this horrible thing. That Eddie's skin was already showing the tell-tale signs of the switch; fur growing on his arms where there had only been hair before. Teeth growing, now too big for his mouth—which was frothing. The jerking as the spasms took him, as the transformation occurred that would heal his wounds but make him something else entirely.

"Doc, let me," said Angel. "While he's still—"

She shook her head. Eddie was her patient, her soldier. It was her place. She drew one of her pistols, placed the barrel in the middle of his forehead, having to burrow in almost to get it to stay. Kingsley sucked in a huge breath, closed her eyes, and pulled the trigger.

Eddie Haines stopped moving. Would never move again.

"Dr Kingsley?" Another voice, not Angel this time. Not Peel either. "We should get moving."

She opened her eyes, hadn't realised she'd had them closed for so long. Angel was already on his feet again, had joined Tommy Daniels who was the person addressing her. Pat was on the other side of him, waiting like a trained lapdog—just like she'd trailed him all this way down. But was that loyalty misplaced? Kingsley wondered, like some kind of parent disapproving of her daughter's boyfriend. None of them had spoken about what had happened when he showed up back at the canteen. Nobody had spoken *to him* about it yet either, regardless of Peel saying he wanted to. Yes, he'd saved them, but . . .

Just how had Tommy done that? What exactly was his connection to the wolves? Was he as dangerous as them?

Then again, if you're going to hang around with Tommy Daniels, sooner or later you're going to end up in hot water . . . You get what you deserve when you get mixed up with him.

There was a hand on her shoulder and she flinched. Peel, bending, showing his support. "I'm okay," she told him, getting up, then facing Tommy: "You're right, we should get moving."

Eddie Haines would never move again. Because of the wolves . . . What was Tommy's connection to the wolves?

Messed up. Fucked up, all of this. Peel, Pat . . . Tommy.

She waited for them to move off but grabbed Peel's arm, pulled him back. "Can . . . can we trust him?" she asked. The safety not only of those she loved was at stake, but everyone who'd followed her down here. Who'd followed Tommy.

Peel stared at her unblinking. Then replied, "I wish I knew, Andrea. I wish to Christ I knew."

CHAPTER SIXTEEN

H E WASN'T JUST COMING NOW, HE'D ARRIVED.

The lift had made its ascent, and the doors were open. Stepping out of them was someone she hadn't seen in over twenty years: the beast, the original beast. Finch, in all his glory: fur bristling, massive and hungry for human flesh. As the doors closed behind him, the lift vanished—the space more closely resembling where this had all begun, centuries ago. That cave in the snowbound wastes.

Was she strong enough? Could she really defeat him this time, put him down again and trap him? She had her list:

Ring . . . no, *save* Tommy. Save everyone.

Do some tidying up around here (this cave is a real pigsty, Rachael!).

Ring Steph and . . . No, Steph was dead—wasn't she?

Get yourself a treat if you win.

Mend a broken heart . . . a broken soul. A broken world.

Could she really do it? The time for such questions was over. This was it, the beginning of the end. The end *game*. She was about to find out, either way. Rachael swallowed dryly, picked up the spear with the glistening tip . . .

And prepared to do battle with her nemesis once more.

CHAPTER SEVENTEEN

Andrea Kingsley had asked him whether Tommy could be trusted.

Now, Noah Peel wasn't sure that he could. As he held the axe in his hand, gripping it more tightly than ever, he was staring past the youth—beyond him and into that room. At what was inside.

"Get out of my way!" he shouted at Tommy.

"Can't do that," came the reply.

"I won't tell you again." Peel was tensing, getting ready to draw back the axe. To sweep Tommy aside if he had to. "She needs to be killed."

"Can't let you do that, either."

It was a simple decision as far as Peel was concerned. If he didn't do this, then everything they'd gone through—all the sacrifices—would have been in vain. Pat was screaming at him that he wasn't thinking clearly, that grief was clouding his judgement, but then weren't her feelings for Tommy doing the same?

"For the love of . . . Look at her!"

"She deserves a chance," Tommy argued. Then more softly, "She's my mother."

Peel pulled a face. That thing sitting there was nobody's mother, not looking the way she did. All it had taken was a glimpse of her—the door to that final room open—and everything had slotted into place. He had to do this, for their memory: the people they'd lost along the way.

Going down, down—deep into the complex. Descending staircases, short hops in lifts. Until they'd arrived at the last one, the one that would bring them down here. The mutts were gaining on them: so many, might even have been all of them. While they themselves were down to the few remaining survivors, all the rest of their team dead. And they had to assume everyone else up above was the same.

Five of them. Angel, Tommy, Pat, Kingsley and him.

"Go! Get inside," Angel had told them, and Peel could see the loyalty for Tommy in that man's eyes. Some kind of debt which had to be repaid. Anyone who commanded that kind of fidelity couldn't be all bad, could he? Then there was the way Pat looked at the guy . . .

"Angel, you'll be—"

"Just go already. I'll hold them off." An impossible task and there was absolutely no hope of surviving, but they'd done as he said—thanking him as Tommy opened those lift doors.

They were just getting inside when the first of the creatures showed up. Angel had fired at them, but was overwhelmed in seconds; one swipe sending him spinning as he was still shooting. The bullets had peppered the lift even as the doors closed.

"Get down!" Peel had warned, pulling on Pat, on Kingsley. Who fell a little too easily. Dropping, like she couldn't stand up anymore. It was only then that Peel saw the blood, stark against the whiteness of the coat she was still wearing. The holes that had punctured her back. Red, so red.

"No . . . *No!*" He'd cradled her there on the floor of the lift, as dogs dropped onto the ceiling and Pat had snatched up the doctor's abandoned rifle to fire up at them; to kill them.

They'd remained like that all the way down, until the lift juddered to a halt. When the doors opened, Tommy had virtually pulled Pat away from the scene. "Let them have a moment," he'd said, and Peel had been grateful for that. Grateful too for having known this woman, however briefly. Not bitter that she was dying in his arms, just thankful for the time they'd spent together.

"Hey . . ." she said to him. "Hey, don't cry." She wiped away the tears from his one good eye with her fingertips. "Big . . . Big Boys like you don't cry. I'm . . ." She coughed, blood appearing on her lips. "I'm in pretty good . . . nick, all things con-considered."

"I . . ." Peel began, but she placed one of those fingertips on his lips.

"Shh . . . Me too. Now . . . now why don't you . . . hand me that bag of grenades you've been carrying . . . around with you, and I'll go . . . go and give those mongrels our best."

"How did you. . . ?" But Peel shook his head. She knew what he'd grabbed back there in the armoury, because she knew *him*. And he knew they might come in handy at some point, probably near the end. He hadn't been wrong.

Peel kissed her, then handed her the bag.

"Go on then," she told him, smiling and nodding. Waiting for him to step through the doors, before reaching up and pressing the button that would take her back up again, waving at him weakly as the doors closed.

He waved back, then almost collapsed against the wall of the corridor. Peel felt hands there, catching him, helping him. Pat, with tears rolling down her own cheeks. Turning him and helping him away from the lift doors, half-carrying him to the other end so that when the explosion came—when the debris fell to the bottom of the lift shaft, bowing it and cutting it off completely—he was safely away from the scene. The lights flickered, then began alternating between normal and crimson.

But that's when he had looked up. That's when he'd seen Tommy in the doorway, peering into the mirrored room through the open door. That's when he'd seen the thing on the seat, clutching that wooden box. Half-woman, half-wolf.

Rachael Daniels, Tommy's mother. Or at least it had been. The woman he'd saved back at the motel, though he hadn't been in time to save her partner. The woman who'd fled, never to be seen again— evading the authorities, evading *him*. The woman who'd known about The First Wolf.

The woman who had been attacked by The First Wolf. Who knew where to find it because she actually *was* that wolf, had been when she'd given birth to Tommy . . .

Can . . . can we trust him?

Flashes of the canteen went through Peel's mind then, how those mutts had parted for Tommy. The connection that must have been there, that must have been the spanner in the works during that last push Grice led—either him or his mother. Tommy had been protecting her all along, keeping her hidden down here. Until the time was right, until the base had been overrun. Had led them all down here to witness the return of their great leader.

Tommy saw that he'd spotted them, held up his hands. "It's not what you think."

"Isn't it?" Peel could barely control the rage that was building up in him.

"She's . . . she's fighting her own battle. She's done it before, we need to give her—"

"We need to end this!" He'd rushed towards that room, hefting his axe.

"Peel . . . Wait, listen to what Tommy has to say!" Pat behind him, but she was so turned around she didn't know what she was talking about.

"It's The First Wolf, Pat. Remember what I said, we can end this. Right here, right now."

He was vaguely aware of noises back down the other end of the corridor where they'd come from, clawing and scratching. Wolves trying to get through. So Andrea hadn't got all of them, and they were still coming. Coming to meet their maker.

"She's my *mum!*" Tommy repeated.

"Look at her, she's a *monstrosity!* " shouted Peel. How could the lad not see that, unless he was a monstrosity himself? Stalling Peel, waiting for the dog part of her to take over completely. Waiting for it to take over him?

Peel shook his head. It needed to be done: for Angel, for Andrea, for his old gaffer in the police force, Moss . . . For everyone who'd died when the wolves rose and took over. Hands were there behind him again, but this time tugging at him, pulling him back.

"Pat, don't—" He turned, and that was when he felt it. The claws in his stomach, digging upwards. Peel dropped his weapon, more out of surprise than anything. He gaped at what had done this. One of the wolves had broken through, obviously, stopped him from hurting their master.

But no. It was Pat, her eyes glazed over red—her hand in his stomach, grinning wildly at his pain.

It was Pat. But how could it be Pat? he asked himself.
How could it be her?

CHAPTER EIGHTEEN

SHE'D FOUGHT VALIANTLY, HARDER THAN HE HAD ANTICIPATED given her condition.

But, in the end, there could be only one outcome. He'd been waiting decades for this, growing more powerful, while she'd just been losing her edge.

"I'm . . . I'm not afraid," she kept repeating over and over, but the crack in her voice said different.

Rachael had thrust with the silver spear, left and right—but he'd dodged it every time, clawing at her arms, her legs. Then her torso and back, spinning her around and around until blood sprayed from her like a sprinkler in a garden.

Then he felled her completely, knocking the weapon out of her hands for good. Her only defence against him. And he'd pinned her there to the ground, had begun to devour her. Just as he had done before, back in a park on the Greenham Estate. She'd taken him by surprise that time, he'd underestimated her will—the desire to stay alive being transferred into him, taking over and subduing his consciousness.

This time *he* was in control. *He* was the one who would be victorious.

Finch had only one thing to say to her, as he bit and chewed: "Temet Nosce, Rachael. Know Thyself."

Know thyself, and know when to quit. It was over.

All this was finally over.

CHAPTER NINETEEN

T OMMY HAD BEEN AS SHOCKED AS ANYONE AT HER SUDDEN TRANS-
formation.

The way Pat had dug into Peel like that, disarming him and practically lifting him off the floor. Something was smoking around her neck; her chain it looked like. Beyond them, at the lift, a piece of rubble fell. A hole opened . . . and a claw appeared. It was all happening too fast for him. The wolves were coming.

No, not wolves: *A* wolf.

One, judging from the look on Peel's face—when he could tear his gaze away from Pat and what was happening to her—that he recognised. Tommy had seen it before too, back at the canteen; the wolf who'd given the silent command for the others to attack, when they'd been keeping their distance from both him and the people he'd been trying to save.

A general. A leader.

It was standing proud now, having squeezed itself through the gap in the detritus. There were other claws, other teeth there, but those wolves stayed where they were. Not needed for this part of the story. Just this one, the one with the streak that now—when the lighting flashed back to normal for a minute or two—actually looked more blue-silver in colour.

The creature was walking towards them, opened its mouth and spoke: "You're wondering how? Is she an imitation? An actor?" Like 'Steph' back at the warehouse, it was a female voice, a woman's voice, and when she laughed it was almost a delicate sound. "Like our master used to be, like *she* wanted to be." The she-wolf pointed beyond them all, at his mother in the room. "Like we all became to honour him."

"What . . . what the fuck . . . is going on?" This was Peel, struggling to get the words out. Desperately trying to fathom out how this girl who'd been as close to him as a daughter could have been one of the monsters all along.

The she-wolf shook her head. "She's very real, I assure you. Which I suppose makes this all the more painful for you. I hope."

Pat twisted her claw into Peel and he let out a cry of pure agony.

"Don't blame her, though. She never knew what she was. It only works if they don't know, you see. It was how your mother got away with her deception to begin with, because she didn't know what she'd done. Then, of course, once she'd imprisoned our Lord, become Rachael again, the mirrors, the tests didn't work anyway. Human, to all extents and purposes . . . Had to be, or she wouldn't have been able to give birth to you, Thomas."

"I-I don't understand," Peel managed.

"Show them, my dear," prompted the wolf, and Pat used her free hand to brush aside the short, spiky hair on one side of her head, just above the ear. There was a tiny scar, almost invisible—but there. A claw wound, the virus held in check there until it was time for her to properly wake up.

"A sleeper agent," gasped Tommy.

"Bingo! Give that man a cigar—to use one of *your* colourful quotes, Mr Peel. Oh, we've been keeping an eye on everything through Pat. Even got her to do little . . . jobs for us, now and again."

"The plans," said Tommy. "Operation Wolfshead."

"She's very good at sneaking around, sneaking into places. That's what made her a good messenger. Then of course, when one of us knows, all of us know . . . including you, Thomas."

That was a relief if nothing else, that he hadn't been to blame for the death of all those men. He'd been beginning to wonder if he could even trust himself.

"This . . . It can't be . . . happening," Peel grunted.

"How did you put it, Mr Peel? Oh yes, 'What's with all this pretending to be something you're not anyway?' Well now she isn't anymore. Now she's exactly what she was always meant to be. Ours."

Another twist of the claw, another scream of torment. Tommy rushed to try and help Peel, finally waking up himself to the fact this wasn't his Pat. But she turned and clipped him with the back of her hand, sending him sprawling against the far wall. Not hard enough to do any real damage, just enough to keep him down while the life ebbed out of the man with the eye-patch.

The she-wolf yawned. "It's been a long couple of days and as amusing as it is to watch Mr Peel squirm, his part in all this is over. Finish what you started."

Looking up, Tommy saw Pat hesitate: a conflicted look wash across her face. But then it was gone and she opened her mouth far wider than it should have been able to open, clamping down on Peel's neck and biting into it. Ripping away a huge chunk of flesh and eating it greedily. His remaining eye rolled back into his head and she let him go, allowing Peel to slump to the floor in a heap.

He whispered one last thing before he died, barely audible but loud enough for Pat to hear—for Tommy to hear it as well. "What's your . . . your name? I'll . . . I'll tell you mine if . . ." But then he was gone. Tommy had no idea what it meant, but he saw another flash of recognition on Pat's face, the words obviously triggering something.

The she-wolf with the blue-silver streak stepped closer, peering down at the dead man. "Shame," she said. "He might have made a good wolf, if he hadn't been so set in his ways. The question now is . . . will you?" One clawed finger was pointing in Tommy's direction.

"Never!" he answered, quickly and firmly.

"We'll see. Oh, this form is making you uncomfortable. I can tell." The she-wolf began to morph into something else then, some*one* else. Tommy stared at her, recalling the woman he was seeing in front of him, remembering her—as he had done with Steph—from photos his mother had kept. "Better?" asked the lady with the blue-rinse hair, who looked old but far from frail.

"You're . . . you're Tilly. Tilly—"

"Brindle. I was, once, yes: the actual, original Tilly Brindle. Well done, young man." She was distracted then in full flow, by something that was happening in the room behind them. The old woman grinned, got on one knee. "Look, it's time! Welcome, sire!" Tommy followed her gaze, and saw it: the shape in the chair.

There was no trace of his mother left, only the wolf. The First Wolf as Peel had called it.

"Well, hello there yourself," it said in a throaty voice. "It's sooo good to be back!"

ᔐ

Finch looked out on the scene in front of him.

The first time he'd properly looked at anything with his own eyes in such a long time. It felt good. And what was he looking at, exactly? Four figures. One was the old lady he'd once savaged and left for dead before taking her place. She was bowing—as it should be—and welcoming him back. One was what looked like a young girl, stuck in mid-transformation, standing over the body of a dead man she'd obviously just killed (Finch had been busy at the time).

The other, also on the floor but starting to rise, was a boy wearing a cap. Thomas Daniels . . . No, Thomas Finch. His son.

"Mu . . . mum?" asked the boy.

"Your mother's dead," he told him flatly. It wasn't the whole truth, but Thomas didn't need to know that right now. Might affect his decision; especially if the lad knew what he had in mind for her. "She died before you were even born."

"No!" he shouted.

"I'm afraid so. She . . . I let her borrow this body for a while. Yes, that's right. I let her borrow it so that you could be born. So, you see, you should be thanking me."

The youth was shaking his head. "No . . . *No!* That's not what happened."

"Anyway, she's gone now. What say you and I have a little fun, Thomas? Would you like that? Catch up on some quality son and dad time?"

"My name's Tommy, and you're *not* my dad," the boy spat. "He was killed by one of your kind."

"Accept it, you came from me. I'm part of you and you're part of me."

"No," repeated the youth, looking horrified.

Finch held out a clawed hand, and said in the most serious voice he could muster: "Come with me, and we can rule this shit-hole world as father and son." Then he laughed, long and hard. "Just my little joke. Where's your sense of humour?"

"I'll never go anywhere with you. Do *anything* with you!"

"Okay, your choice," said Finch, then effected the serious voice again. "If you can't be turned . . . then you must die!" He shook his clawed hand, half expecting lightning to come out, then laughed again. "The first ones were the best of those movies by a country mile. I auditioned for Solo, you know—but that's another story. All right . . . Miss Brindle, would you do the honours?"

"Lord," she said, getting up off her knee. "If I may, the girl."

"Ah right, I'm with you. His little lady. You're right, that might be quite entertaining. Speaking of which . . ." He closed his eyes.

Rachael, I know you're still there . . . a little piece of you anyway. You might want to see this, your boy's about to get his. The person you love the most in this whole, wide world. How about that?

He waited, but there was no reply.

Suit yourself.

Then he nodded, his first order to be carried out since his return. Felt kinda nice. It would be the first of many. His minions had prepared this world for him; no more running, no more hiding. He could walk around it openly without fear of reprisals. It would be fun.

More than that, it was going to be great!

જી

"Well, what are you waiting for? You heard our master, you have your orders!"

Pat had seen, she'd heard. Was moving towards Tommy even—hand . . . claw out to grab him by the throat.

"Pat, this isn't you," he was saying. "Please don't do this! You have to fight it!"

Fight . . . fight not . . .

But she didn't want to, couldn't he see that. It was out of her control, just like killing Peel. (Oh God, what had she done?) She didn't want to kill Tommy; she *adored* him. Yet she had the youth now, was grabbing him, lifting him. Choking him.

"Put some real effort into it!" she heard The First Wolf call from the room, from his throne.

"You heard, use your teeth. Your claws!" Tilly was shouting.

No, thought Pat. *I can't . . . This isn't—*

"*What's your name?*" The last thing Peel had said to her, was trying to tell her to . . .

"Remember," gasped Tommy, feebly trying free himself. "Remember who you are, Pat!"

The chain, the one her mother had given her, the cross burning into her, was still smoking.

"Do it!" snapped Tilly, voice becoming deeper, more gravely. "Do it now, girl!"

"Don't," whispered Pat, then louder: "*Don't* call me girl!" She let go of Tommy and flew at the old woman, before she could change back. Tearing into her with both teeth and claws, as she'd told her to do with Tommy.

"What . . . what's happening?" Pat heard The First Wolf say, assuming he was asking about her traitorous deeds—but something else was going on back there. Something Pat never got a chance to see, because Tilly was assuming her wolf form again, and fighting back: throwing her opponent against the wall. Pat heard, and felt, bones cracking. She was stronger while she was like this, but was still trying to hang on to her humanity—while Tilly had no such qualms.

But still she fought. Even as she was being laid into she fought, as hard as she could. Fighting to stay human, fighting to stay alive, to be with Tommy.

Fighting . . . Just fighting.

CHAPTER TWENTY

"W HAT'S HAPPENING?" FINCH HAD ASKED.

What was happening was, one minute he'd been enjoying himself immensely. Delighted to be back in charge again, watching as the young bitch killed her lover—though not as inventively as he would have liked, it had to be said—the next he'd felt strange, woozy.

He'd looked around at the mirrored walls, and each of them was throwing back a reflection of someone. Different faces that he'd worn in the past, all of them coming back at him at once; along with the memories of the games he'd played wearing them, those he'd killed whilst wearing them. Dozens and dozens, one for every single mirror and then some: shifting, changing.

And he'd felt *her*, the cow that he'd actually invited back to watch, to witness the death of her son. Still fighting him, still trying to weaken him—her love for Tommy fuelling her rage.

"We're not done yet, Finch!" she cried, dragging him back. Dragging his mind back to that cave, to where it all began. Dragging him back to where she was staggering to her feet, where she was still holding that spear he'd once used himself for protection.

"No . . . No, I won't let you," he'd said, and snapped back to reality, to the present. But she was there as well, wrestling with him for control over his body once more. Grabbing at the box she was holding, feeling for the key around her neck and pulling it free, opening the container.

Photos, keepsakes, memories from a life that should have ended when he ate her. "Those won't save you!" he promised her.

But then he saw it, buried underneath everything. Buried deep, something he hadn't known about. The glint of silver and—

She was dragging him back to the cave again, lumbering towards him with the spear. Falling and ramming it into him, letting the momentum of it do the rest. Ramming it so hard into The First Wolf, he howled in pain.

Then back to the present, a hand no longer covered in fur, no sign of claws, reaching into the box: bringing it out. The silver revolver with one silver bullet in the chamber.

Finch tried to stop her, but he was so weak from the spear—the silver spear that was sticking into him, inching closer and closer to his heart.

The barrel was at his temple.

He looked out, but it wasn't through his eyes now: it was through hers. Looked out ahead of him at the fight going on between the Tilly-wolf and the girl...who was losing. Looked out at the youth with the cap on, face a contortion of terror, rushing to try and stop what was about to happen.

But her finger was on the trigger.

"I do know myself, motherfucker," she said, the words coming from his lips but in her voice—because now it was coming from her face. "I'm Rachael, Tommy's mum. Kathleen's daughter. I'm Rachael Elizabeth Daniels . . .

"I'm Red!"

And with that, she pulled the trigger.

⁊

At the very same moment that the gun went off, that the bullet entered her brain, Rachael dragged them both back to the cave a final time.

She made sure the spear was in The First Wolf's heart muscle, twisting it and watching as that monster breathed its last. Then pulling it out again, because she needed to make sure of something.

Rachael looked at the corpse, but in spite of the fact that she was so, so hungry, she did not eat it. Already she was growing stronger, could feel her wounds healing because of the virus that had been passed on to her. A virus that, one day, would infect so many people on Earth.

She needed to make sure that didn't happen, that this ended with her. So she took hold of the spear, lined herself up with the tip. Then she fell onto it, mirroring what she'd done in the real world with the gun; what she'd done in the future.

As it pierced her heart, she fell sideways, slumping onto the body of the now still wolf-corpse.

And she ticked off her final mental 'to do' list, though it had changed a little and there were fewer things on it:

Ring . . . no, *save* Tommy. Save everyone. Tick!

Mend a broken heart . . . a broken soul. A broken world. Tick.

Get yourself a treat if you win.

PAUL KANE

As she lay there dying, she said the last one to herself over and over: Get yourself a treat if you win. Get yourself a treat if you win . . . Get yourself a . . .

EPILOGUE

THE PARK LOOKED SO BEAUTIFUL TODAY, FLOWERS EVERYWHERE. The first proper day of summer.

All you could hear was the sound of children playing, having fun. Including young Seth, being pushed on the swings by his mum and dad. He was having such a good time, the laughter infectious. Growing up so quickly, in the blink of an eye almost.

His mother raised a hand, waving across at her. She was so pretty, growing her hair out more now; abandoning that short cut she'd had for ages. And such a fighter too! The hard time she'd had giving birth to Seth, it brought back memories her own pregnancy. In fact, Trisha reminded her of herself in so many ways. She couldn't have asked for a better daughter-in-law actually. Hopefully Trisha would have an easier time of it with their next one: a girl, they'd just found out.

A second grandchild; she could hardly believe it.

Her son put an arm around Trisha then, drawing her in for a kiss. Didn't seem like five minutes since she'd been doing all this with Tom, and the thought made her smile. Made her take his hand as he sat beside her on the bench. Made her kiss it, and he—in turn—kissed hers.

She'd known it the first time they'd met in that pub, The Forrester's Arms, when Steph—her best friend who'd moved to Australia and was now happily married to some rich banker—had dragged her out even though she hadn't wanted to go. Was miserable in fact because some prat (she couldn't even remember his name) had dumped her. Rachael was glad she'd ventured out now, because she never would have met the love of her life if she hadn't. Even her own mum, Kathleen, had approved in the end—and she was a tough nut to crack, God rest her soul. Yes, he was a little older and there was baggage (a widower, his wife and first son having died in a car crash). But . . . well, when it was right it was right. He'd even supported her with the acting, taking her to auditions when he could—fitting it around his own job as a handyman.

Rachael glanced across now at the other bench, at Trisha's folks. Noah and Andrea were just as lovely as their daughter, and had brought her up well. What could you expect, though, when your dad was a high-ranking police officer and your mother was a doctor? Andrea had even been in the army briefly before she met Noah, but had settled down with him when they decided to start a family and taken a job at the local hospital. Nice people.

Rachael was glad she'd suggested this trip out to the Greenham Estate. It had changed so much since her time here, when she'd been trying to make ends meet as a care worker. When she'd met Tilly, who she still thought of so fondly even though she was long gone. Was probably the reason why she still came here so often. But today wasn't the day for sad memories.

Rachael took in her family again. She couldn't have asked for more. Asked for better . . . In fact, sometimes she wondered if all this wasn't just a little *too* perfect. Like wish fulfilment, or a dream or something. If it was, then Rachael really didn't want to wake up.

There was a scream, and she looked over immediately to see where it had come from. Seth had fallen from the swing, was on the ground in front of it with his mum and dad fussing round.

Tom was up too, so she followed—joining Noah and Andrea at the scene of the crime.

"Here, let me have a look," Andrea was saying, ever the doctor.

"Doesn't look too bad, champ!" Tommy was telling his son, to try and stop him crying. "Just a little graze."

"But . . . but he's cut himself, look." This was Trisha, pointing to the scrape on the kid's bare knee, visible because of the shorts he was wearing. Trish was just as protective of her son as Rachael and Tom had been of their own growing up. Still were.

And Rachael had followed her gaze to the child's knee, to the cut there. To the blood. She blinked, almost remembering something. Half-recalling an actual dream perhaps. Of a big dog—she'd never liked them, not since she was a kid and she'd been bitten. A big dog that was all teeth and claws . . .

She blinked again, and it was gone. Andrea was cleaning up Seth's wound with antiseptic she'd fished out of her handbag, putting on one of those plasters she always carried with her. "They should give you a medal for that one," Noah told him with a wink.

"*Daaaad,*" Trisha said to him, batting the older man playfully on the arm.

He grinned. "What?"

Then they were leading the limping boy away. But Rachael was still there, staring now at the patch of ground where he'd injured himself.

"You coming, sweetheart?" Tom asked, a hand on her shoulder that made her start. "I'm sorry, I didn't mean to . . . We're off to get Seth an ice cream for being so brave."

"What? Oh, yes, of course. Ice cream."

"You never know, if you're lucky I might buy you one too. As a little treat."

Get yourself a treat.

"Yes. Yes, I'd like that," she told him.

"Are you okay?" he asked, frowning, and she nodded, comforted by his arm around *her* shoulders. But in actual fact, as they walked away themselves, she was still thinking about where Seth had fallen. The blood there that he'd spilled, fascinated by it. The smell of it, the texture. The colour:

Which, after all, had been a shade . . .

The very deepest, deepest shade . . .

Of red.

BIOGRAPHIES

PAUL KANE IS AN AWARD-WINNING, BESTSELLING WRITER AND editor based in Derbyshire, UK. His short story collections include *Alone (In the Dark)*, *Touching the Flame*, *FunnyBones*, *Peripheral Visions*, *Shadow Writer*, *The Adventures of Dalton Quayle*, *The Butterfly Man and Other Stories*, *The Spaces Between*, *Ghosts*, the British Fantasy Award-nominated *Monsters*, *Shadow Casting*, *Nailbiters*, *Death*, *Disexistence*, *Scary Tales* and *More Monsters*. His novellas include *The Lazarus Condition*, *RED* and *Pain Cages* (a #1 Amazon bestseller). He is the author of such novels as *Of Darkness and Light*, *The Gemini Factor* and the bestselling *Arrowhead* trilogy (*Arrowhead*, *Broken Arrow* and *Arrowland*, gathered together in the sellout omnibus edition *Hooded Man*), a post-apocalyptic reworking of the Robin Hood mythology. His latest novels include *Lunar* (which is set to be turned into a feature film), the short Y.A. novel *The Rainbow Man* (as P.B. Kane), the critically-acclaimed and award-winning *Sherlock Holmes and the Servants of Hell* from Solaris and *Before* from Grey Matter Press.

He has also written for comics, most notably for the *Dead Roots* zombie anthology alongside writers such as James Moran (*Torchwood*, *Cockneys vs. Zombies*) and Jason Arnopp (*Doctor Who*, *Friday the 13th*, *The Last Days of Jack Sparks*) and as part of the team turning

Clive Barker's Books of Blood into motion comics for Seraphim/ MadeFire. His stand-alone comic *The Disease*, published by Hellbound Media, was also a 2016 Ghastly Award nominated title in the 'One Shot' category. Paul is co-editor of the anthology *Hellbound Hearts* (Simon & Schuster)—stories based around the mythology that spawned *Hellraiser—The Mammoth Book of Body Horror* (Constable & Robinson/Running Press), featuring the likes of Stephen King and James Herbert, *A Carnivàle of Horror* (PS) featuring Ray Bradbury and Joe Hill, and *Beyond Rue Morgue* from Titan, stories based around Poe's detective, Dupin.

His non-fiction books include *The Hellraiser Films and Their Legacy*, *Voices in the Dark* and *Shadow Writer – The Non-Fiction. Vol. 1: Reviews* and *Vol. 2: Articles and Essays*, plus his genre journalism has appeared in the likes of *SFX, Fangoria, Dreamwatch, Gorezone, Rue Morgue* and *DeathRay*. He also co-wrote the afterword to the latest edition of Stephen King's *Night Shift* collection. He has been a Guest at Alt.Fiction five times, was a Guest at the first SFX Weekender, at Thought Bubble in 2011, Derbyshire Literary Festival and Off the Shelf in 2012, Monster Mash and Event Horizon in 2013, Edge-Lit in 2014, Horror-Con, HorrorFest and Grimm Up North in 2015, The Dublin Ghost Story Festival and Sledge-Lit in 2016, plus IMATS Olympia and Celluloid Screams in 2017, as well as being a panellist at FantasyCon and the World Fantasy Convention, and a fiction judge at the Sci-Fi London Film Festival. He is a former Special Publications Editor of the British Fantasy Society and is currently serving as co-chair for the UK arm of the Horror Writers Association.

His work has been optioned for film and television, and his zombie story 'Dead Time' was turned into an episode of the Lionsgate/ NBC TV series *Fear Itself*, adapted by Steve Niles (*30 Days of Night*) and directed by Darren Lynn Bousman (*SAW II-IV*). He also scripted

The Opportunity, which premiered at the Cannes Film Festival, *Wind Chimes* (directed by Brad 'Hallows Eve' Watson and which sold to TV), *The Weeping Woman*—filmed by award-winning director Mark Steensland, starring Tony-nominated actor Stephen Geoffreys (*Fright Night*)—and *Confidence,* directed by award-winning Mike Clarke (*A Hand to Play, Paper and Plastic*) which stars Simon Bamford (*Hellraiser, Nightbreed, Starfish*). His work for audio includes the full cast drama adaptation of *The Hellbound Heart* for Bafflegab, starring Tom Meeten (*The Ghoul*), Neve McIntosh (*Doctor Who*) and Alice Lowe (*Prevenge*), and the *Robin of Sherwood* adventure *The Red Lord* for Spiteful Puppet/ITV, narrated by Ian Ogilvy (*Return of the Saint*). You can find out more at his website www.shadow-writer.co.uk which has featured Guest Writers such as Dean Koontz, Robert Kirkman, Charlaine Harris and Guillermo del Toro.

BARBIE WILDE IS BEST KNOWN FOR PLAYING THE FEMALE CENOBITE in Clive Barker's *Hellbound: Hellraiser II*. She also featured in *Death Wish 3*, *Grizzly II: The Concert* and in the Bollywood blockbuster, *Janbazz*. As a member of the music-dance group Shock, she supported artists such as Depeche Mode, Ultravox, Adam and the Ants and Gary Numan in the early 1980s. Wilde also wrote and hosted eight different music and film review TV programmes in the UK in the 1980s and 1990s.

In 2009, Wilde moved into writing horror and crime with the publication of her first well-received Female Cenobite short horror story, 'Sister Cilice', for the *Hellhound Hearts* anthology, edited by Paul Kane and Marie O'Regan. The publication of her debut diary-of-a-serial-killer novel, *The Venus Complex*, by Comet Press in 2012 prompted America's best-selling horror magazine *Fangoria* to call her 'one of the finest purveyors of erotically charged horror fiction around'. *The Venus Complex* will be released as an audio book in autumn 2018, narrated by *Hellraiser's* Doug 'Pinhead' Bradley.

Wilde's illustrated collection of short horror stories, *Voices of the Damned*, published by SST Publications in 2015, was called 'sensual in its brutality' and 'a delight for the darker senses' in a starred review from *Publishers Weekly*. *Voices of the Damned* was nominated for the Best Horror Story Collection Award by This is Horror, 2015.

Wilde is now collaborating as co-producer and co-screenplay writer with ex-*Fangoria* Editor-in-Chief and director Chris Alexander (*Blood for Irina*, *Female Werewolf*, *Blood Dynasty*) on the feature length horror movie, *Blue Eyes*, based on her short story of the same name.

DAVE MCKEAN HAS ILLUSTRATED AND DESIGNED OVER EIGHTY award winning and ground breaking books and graphic novels including *The Magic of Reality* (Richard Dawkins), *The Homecoming* (Ray Bradbury), *The Fat Duck Cookbook* and *Historic Heston* (Heston Blumenthal), *What's Welsh for Zen* (John Cale), *Varjak Paw* and *Phoenix* (SF Said), *The Savage, Slog's Dad* and *Mouse Bird Snake Wolf* (David Almond), *Arkham Asylum* (Grant Morrison), *Night Shift* (Stephen King), and *Mr. Punch, Signal to Noise, Coraline* and the Newberry and Carnegie Medal winning *The Graveyard Book* (Neil Gaiman).

He has written and illustrated *Cages* (Harvey, Pantera, Ignatz and Alph Art awards), two *Pictures That Tick* volumes of short stories (V+A Book of the Year), an erotic novel *Celluloid*, and *Black Dog: The Dreams of Paul Nash*, a commission by the 14-18 Now Foundation and the Imperial War Museum. The multimedia live performance of *Black Dog* was featured at Tate Britain, the Somme Memorial in Amiens, and many other festivals in Europe and Canada.

Dave has directed five short films and three feature films, *MirrorMask*, *Luna* (Raindance Festival Best British Feature and BIFA awards) and *The Gospel of Us* with Michael Sheen (two Bafta Cymru awards). He is currently editing his fourth feature *Wolf's Child*, adapted from his own play, created with Wildworks Theatre Company and performed for the Norwich Theatre Festival and at the Trelowarren Estate in Cornwall.

He is Director of Story at the 3-Michelin star The Fat Duck in Bray, and has created murals and packaging for Heston's restaurants in London and Australia.

His work is in private and public collections around the world, and he continues to insist that narrative has a crucial place in art.

His next publishing projects to be released are *Joe Quinn's Poltergeist* with David Almond, *A Suicide Bomber Sat in the Library*, a book backed by Amnesty International with author Jack Gantos, a book of Venice drawings, a long graphic novel inspired by the expressionist classic of German silent cinema *The Cabinet of Dr. Caligari*, and a narrative project for the Louvre in Paris.

CPSIA information can be obtained
at www.ICGtesting.com
Printed in the USA
BVHW031707161118
533315BV00001B/20/P